Anne Manning

Belforest

A tale of English country life. Vol. 1

Anne Manning

Belforest
A tale of English country life. Vol. 1

ISBN/EAN: 9783337174590

Printed in Europe, USA, Canada, Australia, Japan

Cover: Foto ©Andreas Hilbeck / pixelio.de

More available books at **www.hansebooks.com**

BELFOREST.

A

TALE OF ENGLISH COUNTRY LIFE.

BY THE AUTHOR OF

"MARY POWELL," AND "THE LADIES OF BEVER HOLLOW."

IN TWO VOLUMES.

VOL. I.

LONDON:

RICHARD BENTLEY, NEW BURLINGTON STREET.

1865.

CONTENTS.

CHAPTER VII.

PAGE

CHAPTER VIII.

CHAPTER IX.

CHAPTER X.

CHAPTER XI.

CHAPTER XII.

CHAPTER XIII.

CHAPTER XIV.

CONTENTS.

CHAPTER XV.

CHAPTER XVI.

CHAPTER XVII.

CHAPTER XVIII.

CHAPTER XIX.

CHAPTER XX.

BELFOREST.

CHAPTER I.

THE VILLAGE POST-OFFICE.

CLIP-CLOP, clip-clop, clip-clop. Michael Saffery is stamping the letters for the night post. He has already closed the shutters of his little drapery-shop; the bright brass kettle is singing on the hob in the little back-parlour, a buttered muffin is basking before the fire, and he is cosily shut in for the night. I wish every one had as snug a berth!

That buttered muffin is not for Mr. Saffery; it has been toasted by a little girl of remarkably prim demeanour, who is now spreading the tea-table of the lodger. Mr. Saffery's parlour is behind the shop; but the lodger's parlour, which is larger, is parallel with the shop, and looks into the village street. This street, a very devious one, of considerable width, meanders up a hill and then meanders down the opposite side of it, dodging the declivity a little. It is the only street in the village, though there are one or two populous lanes and a green encircled with homesteads. Opposite Mr. Saffery's shop the street has a wide reach or bay, with a little knoll or islet off the opposite coast, wooded by a hoary oak with a seat round it. Under the lee of this oak is the village inn—the "Swan"—where, at this moment, a farmer's cart bound for the beast-market is baiting; it is full of calves calling piteously on their mothers; the air is filled with the incessant, melancholy plaint. Also, the tinkling bell of a muffin-boy from a neighbouring town, a man calling "Live shrimps," and several barking dogs and squeaking pigs prevent any approach to silence. Yet how different from London noises!

The lodger's parlour is scantily furnished, but filled to repletion with his own belongings. The little girl has once already had the privilege of dusting them, and she has eyed them with intense curiosity and interest. There are books, a strange medley; portfolios, sketch-books, paints, easel, palette, and all the apparatus of an artist.

The young man is straining his eyes to read the "Life of Nollekens," by the waning light. As the queer little sprite flickers about the table, he eyes her furtively, with some curiosity, and at length says abruptly—

"I say, little one, how old are you?"

In a very staid manner, she answers,

"Thirteen, sir."

"Thirteen? Why you don't look eleven!"

"No, sir; I'm aware I'm very small of my age" (with a deep sigh). "Some people think I shall never grow again."

This was said as if all the faculty had been consulted about it.

"Why should they think that?"

"I've had a serious illness, sir. A fever. And it settled on my nerves. That's why I'm away from boarding-school."

"Ha! Well, I dare say you'll be better some day. What's your name?"

"Nessy."

"Jessy? Bessy?"

"No, sir, Nessy."

"What a queer name! Why could not your parents call you Jessy or Bessy?"

"My parents had nothing to do with it," said Nessy, looking deeply wounded. "My godfather and godmothers gave me that name—at least *one* of my godmothers did, who left me a fortune!"

"Oh, my goodness! So you're an heiress! To the tune of what?"

"Sir," said Nessy, with severity, "I have *thirty pounds a year*—shall have, at least, when I'm of age; if I live as long—which perhaps I shall not. And that's why I'm being brought up like a lady; for it is all laid out on me."

"And why does a lady wait on my table?"

"Oh," said Nessy, looking pleasantly at him for the first time with her dark-blue eyes, which were very pretty, "it's no trouble, it's a pleasure. I—"

At this moment a sound in the other parlour made her start, as if she were shot, and then dart out of the room. The artist thought he heard the kettle boiling over, and a hasty ejaculation of "O my!" from the pseudo-young lady. An instant after, something whisked past the window, in what appeared to him the aforesaid young lady's shabby black silk frock.

As it was now quite too dark to read, he began to be impatient for tea and candles, which seemed unnecessarily delayed, and rang the bell.

In sailed Mrs. Saffery, a fresh-coloured, comely woman, with the lighted candles in highly-polished candlesticks, not of the precious metals, but borne on a waiter with equal distinction. She drew down the blind and withdrew. Then Nessy brought in the hot tea-pot, and then the—or, at least, *a* hot muffin. The lodger observed she had been crying.

" What was the matter just now ? " said he.

" The matter," said Nessy, reluctantly, " was that the kettle boiled over the muffin, and completely spoiled it ; but I knew the muffin-boy was only at the other end of the village, so I ran after him and got another; only my mamma says—"

And, suppressing a little sob, she withdrew, and appeared no more that night. The artist pitied the poor child, who had probably been chidden for gossiping with lodgers instead of minding her own business; but he did not give it a second thought, diverting himself with his book during tea and while the table was being cleared, and employing himself with pencil and pen during the remainder of the evening. His name was Leonard Antony— Leonardo his comrades laughingly called him. He was now in country quarters while his town lodgings were being painted. Of course, an artist never goes into country quarters of any description without finding something or other to enrich himself with in the way of new materials. This very morning, Mr. Antony had noted a couple of curiously-carved oaken stools in a cottage, and, while sketching them, had been told they were used at funerals to rest the coffin upon while the service was being read. He came upon some quaint memorials, too, of Cardinal Wolsey, and he spent the evening in writing down what he had heard of him, and in finishing his sketch of Wolsey's well.

At dead of night Mr. Antony was roused from sound sleep by a voice loudly bawling under his window—

"Michael Saffery! Michael Saffery!" and,

concluding it could be for nothing short of murder, fire, or thieves, he sprang out of bed and began by hitting his head violently against the bedpost. At the same time, a creaking window was thrown up in the adjoining room and speedily shut down again, and, after some gruff mutterings, silence ensued. Mr. Antony rubbed his head, supposed all was right, and went to bed again.

Next morning, when he entered his parlour, he saw Nessy, with her back to him, immersed in one of his books. Without ceremony, he took it out of her hand, saying—

"Do you know that you should not meddle with what is not yours ?"

She started violently, and said, "I should not have hurt it, sir."

"That's as may be ; at any rate, it might hurt you."

"I don't think it would," she said, regretfully. "It was a very pretty story."

"Ay ; but, my good girl, it is anything but a pretty trick to touch what does not belong to you. I'm a very particular gentleman, and if I find I can't leave my things about without their being meddled with, I shall go away."

Nessy looked sorry and ashamed. She said,

"I promise you, sir, I won't do so any more. It did not occur to me it was wrong, and I'm so fond of reading."

"Yes, but you must confine yourself to books that are given you."

"*Given?*" Nessy's tone implied that in that case she should have none.

"Or lent," said Mr. Antony, sitting down to his breakfast.

Nessy went for the kettle; and, when she had brought it, she said, very humbly—

"I'm sure, if you lent me that book just to finish, I would take the greatest care of it—"

"To finish? Why, how much have you read already?"

"Nearly to the end, sir."

"Oh well, then," said Mr. Antony, almost gruffly, "you may take it away, and make an end of it while I am at breakfast; but mind you bring it back, and don't meddle with any other books of mine, nor even ask for them."

"Very well, sir. Thank you." And away she went with "Paul and Virginia."

When she brought it back, he said, "Well, have you finished it?"

“ Yes, sir,” with a little sigh.

“ It did not end very happily, you see.”

“ No, sir.”

And then, after a minute’s silence, as she swept away the crumbs, she added, reflectively—

“ Virginia was very rich.”

“ Rich ! yes, but it did not make her happier, you see, but quite the contrary,” said Mr. Antony, delighted at the unexpected opening for a moral.

“ We can’t tell what she might have done if she had not been drowned,” said Nessy.

“ No, Nessy ; but take my word for it, that riches do not, of themselves, make people happy.”

“ Should not you like to be rich, sir ? ”

“ Well, that’s a poser,” said he, laughing a little. “ We can’t get on very well without some money, but too much of it is bad for us ; it’s a great responsibility, for which we shall be called to account, whether we think so or not.”

“ But if we use it well,” suggested Nessy.

“ Ay, *then* indeed,” said he, with a shrug and a smile ; and the little maiden, seeing he did not mean to say any more, went away.

"Ten to one," thought he, as he got his painting apparatus together, "that child intends to do great things with her thirty pounds a year. To her it probably seems as considerable an income as I should think a thousand. Should not I like to be rich, indeed! I believe I should!" And he set to work with all his might.

At supper-time the alarm of the previous night occurred to him, and he said to Mrs. Saffery, as she waited on him—

" By-the-bye, what was the meaning of that tremendous uproar last night? I thought the house must be on fire."

" Oh, did you hear it, sir ? " said Mrs. Saffery, looking rather conscious.

" Hear it ? I must have been deaf if I did not."

" Well, sir, you see it was the guard, come for the letters. It's an awkward time of night, and Saffery can't be always sitting up for him, so he makes up the bag before bedtime and takes it up to his room, and lets it down through the window with a string."

" When he happens to wake."

" Oh sir, he always wakes first or last."

" Well, I hope to-night it will be first. It's *my* turn to sleep, this time."

Mrs. Saffery said she knew she ought to apologize. She wished Saffery did not sleep so heavy.

" Could not you wake him ? "

" Well, sir, you see, I sleep heavy too. I've got used to it, so it makes no impression—at first, that is. But we always hear it, soon or late."

" If you did not, I suppose you'd lose your situation ? "

" Oh, sir, it could never come to that. We *always* hear it, soon or late."

" I wonder the guard has patience."

" He hasn't, sir ! He curses and swears."

" Humph ! no wonder."

" It's trying, I know," said Mrs. Saffery, " but when people work hard, they sleep heavy."

" That little girl of yours does not seem to work hard. Why don't you let *her* let down the letters ? "

" Nessy, sir ? Oh, she's such a tender plant !

You've no idea! The night air through the
open window would kill her out of hand."

"Well, I suppose it might—she doesn't look
very strong."

"No, sir, Nessy is far from strong. She's a
great anxiety. She took on so at school that it
gave her a nervous fever."

"Were they cruel to her?"

"No, sir, no; they were kind enough. But
she worritted herself to learn more than she
could learn — she has such ambition, has
Nessy."

"Oh, indeed. She told me she was a young
lady of property."

"Ah, that's child's talk, sir. Thirty pounds
a year *does* seem a fortune to a girl of thirteen,
that has but twopence a week pocket-money;
but, dear me, thirty pounds is little enough to
dress and educate her upon, let alone extras.
And the extras, sir, I do assure you, at these
genteel schools, just double the account!"

"No doubt of it."

"When I found that," said Mrs. Saffery, " I
knew we could not afford extras to Nessy, and
I proved it to her in black and white, for she's
a reasonable child; and she saw it could not

be. But as her aunt had laid it down strict that she was to be a lady, she couldn't abear to be ignorant of anything a lady should know. And so she got doing one thing and another for her schoolfellows, over and above her own tasks, helping them with their sums, mending their gloves and stockings for them, and such like, all in an obliging way, to get them to teach her something in return that they learnt of the masters. And so she got a little draw-ing of one, and a little music of another, all in play-hours, you know, sir, and hindered her-self of her natural recreation and rest, which every child, to be healthy, wants ; and her mind always on the full stretch, anxious-like. But the end of it was, that poor Nessy broke down, and instead of getting ahead, had to give up learning entirely, which was a sore grief and disappointment to her. And so, as she was getting no good at school, we thought it a needless expense ; and had her home to take the run of the house and get well."

"Much the best thing you could do," said Mr. Antony. "And you know, Mrs. Saffery, that it is not playing and drawing that makes the lady. A lady may be a lady and do neither. A woman may be no lady, yet do both."

But Mrs. Saffery shook her head, and withheld her assent to this proposition.

CHAPTER II.

NESSY'S TROUBLE.

" I NEEDN'T have been cross to the queer little
thing," thought Antony. " She shall have the
run of my books, barring Nollekens, if she likes
—though I question if she will find anything
she can understand. At any rate, the prohibi-
tion shall be removed."

So, at breakfast-time, he said, " I will lend
you my books, one at a time, since you are fond
of reading, except the one I am reading myself;
but only on condition of your doing them no
injury."

Nessy's face shone with pleasure. She
thanked him, and, to his surprise and amusement, laid her hand at once and without hesitation on a volume which doubtless had already
attracted her.

" What is it ? " said Mr. Antony. " Oh!
Mrs. Graham's 'Journal of Three Months'

Residence in the Mountains East of Rome.' Yes, read that and welcome."

So, for the rest of the morning, Nessy was supremely happy; for, having performed her customary tasks of dusting, washing up, &c. she, with her mother's concurrence, took the book, carefully covered in newspaper, to a certain lath construction, garlanded with scarlet-runners, dignified by the name of "the arbour," which to her on the present occasion was a veritable bower of bliss. Soon she was, in imagination, exploring Poli and Palestrina, enjoying pleasure parties among old Roman remains, and witnessing country sports and rustic feasts. Soon she was devouring the stories of the brigands, thirteen of whom kept in terror a town of twelve hundred inhabitants—I have not read the book since I was about Nessy's age, but I remember it all as vividly as yesterday—how banditti carried off a poor surgeon named Cherubini, and threatened his life unless his family sent an enormous ransom—how the shepherds were in league with the brigands—how the robber chief quarrelled with one of his prisoners and slew him—how a handful of soldiers and the bravest of the townspeople went in pursuit of the brigands and came upon their lair while it was yet warm—all this and much more did Nessy read with avidity, and realize the better inasmuch as there were illustrations of the narrative by Eastlake's graphic pencil. Having finished it all too soon, she sat in a maze, her head resting on her hands, living it over again. Then she thought what a pity it was she could not keep the book to read over and over whenever she liked, and it occurred to her that the next best thing to possessing it would be to copy it.

No sooner said than attempted. Nessy flew into the house for an old ledger her father had given her, in which she had already inserted many ill-written exercises. Providing herself with this *tome*, and with pen and ink, she returned to the arbour; her facile mother being satisfied that she must be doing herself good as long as she was in the open air.

And thus, returning to the house only for her dinner, Nessy spent the whole afternoon, industriously and happily, but gradually getting feverish over her work, and writing worse and worse. It was her grand ambition (Mrs. Saffery had said Nessy was ambitious) to finish

Cherubini's letter before the early tea-hour; but this she almost despaired of doing; especially as, in the over-haste, which is worst speed, she had made sundry omissions, which necessitated interlineations, sadly marring the neatness of her manuscript.

"One page more only," thought she, rapidly dipping her pen.

At that moment, her mother, at the garden-door, sharply called, "Nessy!" making the poor, nervous girl start from head to foot; and oh, woe! a round, black drop of ink fell on the page of Mr. Antony's book.

The complicated terrors of the event presented themselves at one glance to Nessy. There was the book spoilt! There was her promise that it should not be injured broken! How could she tell him? What would he think of her? Could she sop the ink up? No, it was already dry. There stood the ineffaceable spot, like the drop of blood on Lady Macbeth's hand.

An evil suggestion darted through her mind. Should she shut up the book and return it without saying anything about it, trusting to its never being discovered? That suggestion only presented itself to be rejected. It was a great point in Nessy's life. To you, to me, the dilemma may appear trivial; it did not seem so, it was not so, to her. Oh, no! it was a very serious crisis; but, happily, she at once decided virtuously; and as she did so, the hot tear it cost her fell on the blot, but without effacing it. She carefully wiped away the tear, and, deeply sighing, closed the book and carried it indoors. As she entered the house, Mrs. Saffery said, more crossly than was her wont,—

"Nessy, there are but few things you have to do, and I expect you to do them. Mr. Antony has rung twice, and I have had to leave my clear-starching to carry in his tea, because you were out of the way. Take in his muffin."

"Yes, mother." She carried it in sadly; then, after a moment's pause, said, in an unsteady voice, "I'm sorry, sir, I must return you your book."

"Why so?" said Mr. Antony, in surprise.

"Because I've blotted it."

"The deuce you have!" said he, hastily. Her pale face became very red.

"How came you to do so?" continued Mr.

Antony, taking the book from her roughly, and running the leaves through his fingers.

Nessy could hardly command her voice, but, seeing that he could not find the place, she said, " I'll show you, sir," and found it.

" Ho !—humph ! Yes, it's a bad job, certainly ! Serves me right for lending books to little girls that don't know how to use them."

Nessy's heart swelled.

" You've made it worse, too, by trying to wash it out."

" No, sir, no ! "

" What makes it so wet, then ? "

" Sir, it was only a— "—and other tears rolled down.

" Only a tear, do you mean ? " said he, softened.

Nessy nodded : she could not speak.

" Well, it's no good crying. The mischief's done."

" Yes ! I'm so very, *very* sorry ! "

" Come, you needn't cry any more about it. Only you can't expect me to lend you any more books."

" Oh, no, sir ! No, indeed ! "

" How came you to be meddling with ink ?
What were you doing with it ? "

" Copying it."

" *Copying* it ?   Copying what ? "

" The book, sir."

Mr. Antony looked much inclined to laugh.

" Do you really mean you liked this book
so much that you were going to copy it out,
right through ? "

" Yes, sir, great part of it."

" Why, it never would have repaid your
time and trouble."

" Oh ! " said Nessy, " the trouble was a
pleasure, and my time is of no value."

" Go and fetch this precious performance of
yours.   I think it must be a curiosity."

Nessy, much relieved at the turn the dialogue
had taken, hastened to obey his directions, and
soon returned, carrying the ledger.

" I know it's very badly done," said she,
apologetically.

" Yes," said he, after a pause, during which
he had looked through what she had been
writing, " it *is*, as you say, badly done—*very*
badly. Of course, your chief object was to
secure the contents of the book (why it should

interest you so much I know not), and for that purpose any readable writing would do, though I can hardly call this readable. However, I suppose you can read it yourself."

" Oh, yes, sir ! "

" Well, Nessy, considering how you aspire to be a lady, I think you might aspire to write a better hand. Your mother can hardly believe —what is quite true, however—that music and drawing will not, of themselves, make a lady, and that a lady may be a lady who knows neither ; but a lady can hardly be a lady who does not write a good hand. *No* lady would write such a hand as this. It is what used to be called, when I was a little boy, a chandler's-shop hand ; but in these days of education, chandler's-shop people write very good hands, and would be quite ashamed of writing like this. Take my advice, therefore, and try to write better, whether you aim at being a lady or not."

" Yes, sir," said Nessy, softly, and looking much humiliated.

" And as for this book—ahem—you may finish reading it, since you have begun it, if you will not make any more blots."

"I *have* finished it, sir, thank you."

"What! all through? I see you have attempted to preserve it, too, by covering it with newspaper. Well, we won't say any more of this blot, especially as you came and told of it at once (not but what I should have been safe to find it out). But, as for lending you any more, I really don't think I have any here that you would care to read."

"Oh, sir, I don't expect such an indulgence."

"But would it *be* an indulgence?"

"Yes, certainly, sir."

"What would you like to have, supposing I suffered myself to be prevailed upon to be so very weak and soft as to make trial of you again?"

Nessy saw he was not at all cross now, so she at once put her finger, smiling and silently, on the corner of the "Life of Nicholas Poussin."

"Well," said Mr. Antony, "I think you'll find yourself disappointed in it; but, however, you may try. But no ink, Nessy, this time, if you please. If you copy, it must be in pencil."

"Oh, yes, sir; I wish I had done so before. It is very good of you to trust me."

And away she went, happy as a queen, yet with a nervous catch in her breath, like the ground-swell after a storm: and when she remembered what a shock and temptation and struggle were safely overpast, she could not help her eyes from filling with tears.

But she felt very thankful that she had been carried safely through it; and very grateful to Mr. Antony for being so placable and benignant. I repeat it; this was a point in Nessy's life—a crisis that helped to form her character. Seeming trifles, such as these, are sometimes very important to little people; and to great people too.

"Poor little wretch!" thought Mr. Antony, as he ate his muffin, "she was properly frightened, if ever child was. An honest little creature, too, to come and tell of it as she did, instead of waiting to be found out. What a funny fancy of hers, to copy all that! What was there in it that she was taken with, I wonder? To me the narrative seemed trite enough. But I suppose her own imagination dressed it up for her, somehow—just as mine did Sir Robert Ker Porter's campaign in Russia, which now I can't for the life of me see any charm or spirit in. Sometimes the sunshine illumines a landscape, and gives it, for the moment, a beauty not its own."

CHAPTER III.

"WHY DON'T HE WRITE?"

IT is curious how hunger will find palatable and wholesome nutriment in food that in ordinary circumstances we should consider uninviting. Not to speak of the Esquimaux relish for tallow candles and soap, we know that necessity compelled the Huguenots to the preparation of tripe, the French soldiers in the Crimea cooked dainty dishes of nettles, and the German peasants rejoice in daisy and dandelion salads. Appetite is a good sauce. Just so with books. Hunger for new and vivid impressions makes us hunt them out where most unlikely to be found. As a child, I used to delight in forty-eight numbers of the *Edinburgh Review,* from which I culled many a graphic extract and false impression ; and it is curious to remember now, how, while adopting unquestioningly its canons of criticism, and considering it beyond doubt that "the Lake poets" must be very silly men, I devoured every scrap that was vouchsafed of the Lake poetry.

In like manner, Nessy fed, not so much on what she would as what she could ; and, failing any more such dreamy romances as " Paul and Virginia," was fain to content herself with " Nicholas Poussin." Nor was it difficult : Nessy was in the habit of forming pictures to herself ; and here were pictures by the dozen ; not portrayed, indeed, but described.

What had attracted her to the book were two of Fenelon's " Dialogues of the Dead," in the appendix ; for children love easy dialogue. These dialogues were between Poussin and Parrhasius. She did not know who Parrhasius was, nor who Poussin, but she had before her the means of resolving the latter question. As for the banks of the Styx, she had learnt a mythological catechism at boarding-school, and read Butler's Astronomy in class, so she was at least as well up in that department as most real young ladies. Far more vivid was the pleasure she took in it ; for Nessy, unconsciously, had something of the temperament of a poet; and even our best, most Christian poets, find themselves glad, somehow, to trick allusion and metaphor in the old Greek fable.

These dialogues, then, were nuts to Nessy; and many a true and false canon of art did she derive from them. A new world was opening to her; she had scarcely seen a picture, and yet now her mind was full of pictures. After the dialogues came a descriptive catalogue of Poussin's paintings. She formed images of them all. Such passages as the following, for instance, were vividly suggestive.

" No man, perhaps, ever equalled him in the choice of subjects, or in the happiest moment in which to seize his history—as in the saving of Pyrrhus. The rebels have just reached the party, and are seen fighting with the guards of the young prince: the Megarians, on the other side of the river, beckoning, show that there is a probability of safety; but there is still enough of uncertainty to give interest and action to the piece. None better than Poussin knew how to excite the passions and affections."

" 'Moses exposed.' Jochebed is placing the cradle of bulrushes carefully on the river's brink, near a recumbent statue of Nile leaning on a sphinx. Her husband has turned away, and little Aaron follows him. Miriam stands by her mother, and makes signs that some one is approaching. Nothing can be more expressive than all these figures; behind them are some fine trees, at the foot of one of which there is an altar covered with offerings, and on the branches are hung a bow and quiver, and some musical instruments; through the trees, a majestic city, partly composed of local views of Rome." (I regret to say that this incongruity did not strike Nessy.)

" 'The Finding of Moses.' The princess here has seven attendants, besides a man in a boat, who appears to have been employed in saving the child. The Nile and sphinx occupy a portion of the foreground. . . . In the background are persons in a boat, engaged in hunting the hippopotamus, an incident taken from the Prænestine pavement."

" 'Moses trampling on the Crown of Pharaoh.' Pharaoh, seated on a couch, has his crown lying by him, on which Moses, apparently two years old, treads. The priests, considering this an evil omen, one of them is about to stab the child, who is saved by a female attendant ; the princess and her women taking part. The background is very simple ; it is a wall, over which appears a single palm-tree, and the upper part of a temple of the Ionic order."

The following were, with equal industry, copied in pencil.

" 'Achilles discovered by Ulysses.' While Ulysses appears only intent on selling the contents of his box of pedlar's ware, and is offering a diadem to Deidamia, Achilles has seized a sword, and is eagerly drawing it from the scabbard."

" 'Young Pyrrhus saved.' This is one of the most celebrated of Poussin's works. The story is admirably told. Æacidas, king of Molossis, having been driven from his kingdom by rebels, his two friends, Angelus and Androclides, fled with his infant son Pyrrhus and his nurses. The enemy pursued them so closely that the same night they came up with them on the banks of a river, swollen by recent floods. Finding it impossible to ford the stream, one of them wrote a few lines on the bark of a tree, and tying them to his spear, threw it to the opposite bank, to ask the assistance of the

Megarians. They tied trees together to make a raft, and saved the prince. The moment Poussin has chosen is that in which the Megarians are prepared to receive Pyrrhus and his friends : the enemy is at hand ; the terror of the women is lively, the friendly strangers beyond the river are making signs to them to cross it. One of them uses the common modern manner of beckoning in use among the Romans at this day, and as it is probable that they have retained more antique customs than other nations, he has shown his judgment in adopting that action."

This was an epic—the next was an idyl. I know some one who has quite as much pleasure in copying it as Nessy had.

" 'Arcadian Shepherds.' The thought in this picture has been greatly and justly praised. Two Arcadian shepherds and a shepherdess are looking on the inscription on a tomb in the midst of an agreeable landscape. The inscription carries the moral—it is simply, *I, too, dwelt in Arcadia.*"

"I, too, dwelt in Arcadia." Nessy, if her feelings had been thoughts, could have echoed those words. The book took her quite out of and away from herself—made her now and then give great sighs.

She began the painter's life with reverence, and found it interested her less than she had expected and wished. She pitied him for being recalled from his beloved Rome to the French court, to be employed in trifles, and sympathized with him in his joy when he got back. One or two sage axioms fixed themselves in her retentive memory. "'As I grow older,' wrote Poussin to a friend, 'I feel myself more than ever inspired with the desire of surpassing myself, and of attaining the highest degree of perfection.' It has been observed that where a sound mind and body have remained, painters have improved, even to extreme old age. Titian improved to the last, and he died of the plague at ninety-seven."

There was something pleasant in the idea that one might go on improving to the age of ninety-seven.

After reading so much about painting it was natural that she should aspire to bring theory into practice. One day, when Mr. Antony returned to dinner, he saw Michael Saffery standing at his shop door, with a very compla-

cent expression of countenance, which was re-
flected on the faces of his wife and daughter
who stood on either side of him. Their heads
bobbed up and down as they alternately looked
across the road and then at a small white paper
Michael Saffery held in his hand; but as soon
as Nessy saw Mr. Antony, she vanished out of
sight.

"This isn't exactly bad, sir, is it?" said
Michael Saffery to the artist as he approached,
at the same time handing him the paper. The
first sight of it nearly threw Mr. Antony into
fits; it was so difficult to avoid an explosion of
laughter, which, had he yielded to, would have
deeply wounded the parental feelings. Nessy
had drawn the view from the attic window on
the horizontorium principle; so that, if you
could not see round four sides of a square cube,
you certainly could see three, and the effect was
most grotesque. Again, the groups of figures,
not sparsely introduced, were truly Chinese,
almost more alive than life. Mr. Antony,
controlling his muscles by a violent effort, pronounced the single word "capital," and passed
on into his room, leaving his host impressed
with a conviction that he was very laconic.

Nessy was too conscious to wait at table that day; though she might have done so with impunity, for, after the first minute, Mr. Antony never bestowed a thought on her performance.

There was a poor woman, dressed in shabby black, who used to come almost daily to the post-office with the same inquiry—

"Please, sir, is there a letter for me from my son George?"

And when Mr. Saffery replied in the invariable negative, she as invariably rejoined—

"Dear me, why don't he write?"

To this, Mr. Saffery would gravely reply that perhaps he had no pen, ink, and paper, or no stamp, or was a long way from a post-office, or on a journey, or too busy, or had nothing to say, or had no mind to write. To these varied conjectures she would sometimes reply querulously—

"But he's gone to the gold-diggings—he might send me a money-order."

Mr. Saffery would answer by a little shrug and shake of the head, or sometimes put her off with—

"Perhaps he will write by the next mail."

On which she would look wistfully in his

face for a little while, then give a deep sigh and withdraw.

Mr. Antony had heard her make the inquiry one day, and, being struck by the humour rather than the pathos of it, had echoed her words when Mrs. Saffery brought in his supper, saying—

"Well, Mrs. Saffery, have you brought me a letter from my sister?"

And when she said "No, sir,"

"Why don't she write?"

It was one of the privileges of lodging at the post-office, that instead of getting his second-delivery letters at breakfast-time, he had them overnight; that is, when there were any to have. But, like all forestalled pleasures, this sometimes only forestalled disappointment; for he knew all the sooner that he had no letters to receive.

After one or two trials of this sort, he was rewarded by Mrs. Saffery's coming in to him with her pleasantest smile, saying, "A letter, sir," and handing it to him on a waiter with very little japanning left on it. He smiled too. It was a nice, fat little packet, directed in a pretty, ladylike hand; so he settled himself in the most comfortable posture for enjoying it, snuffed the candles and began.

"My dear Leonard,　　　　　Jones Street, *May* 16.

"I had nothing particular to write about yesterday, and did not feel very well, so I thought I would wait till to-day. The paint made me feel rather sick, in spite of what I said to you, so I took your advice at last and came here, where Miss Hill is very glad to receive me. The men were off work yesterday, so the second coat was not put on as promised, and this, of course, will occasion a little more delay. I am sorry to say my little story is 'declined with thanks.' I suppose the editor's hands are full. So it did not much signify that there was a difference of five pounds in our estimates of its value. Mr. Penguin does *not* take your 'Sunshine—Storm coming on.' He says there are so many. Not with the same effect, though, *I* think. It will be sure to sell, soon or late ; good pictures always do. Hit off some bright little thing for the next exhibition, such as will be sure to please—a young mother with her child, or something of that sort,—without fretting over unsuccessful efforts already made, and trying to force them down.

"It came into my head last night, as I was lying awake, that it is nonsense for people to say such and such a thing is hackneyed. Nothing is hackneyed to real genius. Of course, if Shakspeare were to come to life again, and sit down to write on any or all of the subjects now called hackneyed, he would turn out something perfectly fresh. Set one of our great essayists to write on some trite theme—on Truth—on Honour—on Fame—he would produce something perfectly new, something we wondered we had never thought of saying ourselves. And so with everything else. Therefore do not fancy, my dear Leonard, as you do sometimes when you are dispirited, that all the good subjects are taken up. They may all be used over again in a new way; and there are hundreds of others besides. I am sorry for this little disappointment of yours, because I know you were rather in want of the money; but I have carefully gone over last month's expenses, and they were just sixteen-pence halfpenny less than the month before, and even then, you know, we were living within our means.

Your affectionate sister,

Edith Antony."

CHAPTER IV.

A MISUNDERSTANDING.

THIS letter did not enliven Mr. Antony. It was a short one: what made the envelop so fat was that it also enclosed a boot-maker's bill; on seeing which, he muttered, " Bother ! "

He sighed. Old Penguin had seemed so likely to buy that " Sunshine—Storm coming on ;" and now he said " there were so many." So many what? Storms coming on? Very likely. Stupid old fellow. *Stingy* old fellow. *He*, fancy he knew a good picture !

" ' Hit off some bright little thing for the next exhibition.' That's cool of you, Miss Edith. Suppose I were to advise you to hit off some bright little thing for the *Cornhill, Macmillan,* or *Fraser.* ' Declined with thanks.' *Don't* they thank one? Well, it's best to be civil. Poor little Edith ! that's a disappointment to her, I know. It's a shame they won't have it: that story of hers is worth a dozen of the washy, flashy things they print—for washy, flashy readers. Humpty-dumpty sat upon a wall. Ay, and got a great fall; there's a moral in that, my masters. Aim highly, fall nobly. But I'd rather not fall.

> " 'Fain would I climb, but that I fear to fall.'
> ' If thy heart fail thee, do not climb at all.'

" Ha, ha—capital ! Almost as good as—"

> " 'My grief is great, because it is so small.
> Then were it greater, if 'twere none at all ! '

" Query, is that a sequitur ? Heigho, I'm as flat as a fish. Why could not the girl say a word about Rosabel ? Probably because she had not a word to say."

In this disjointed fashion did Mr. Antony pursue his cogitations till Mrs. Saffery came in to clear the table. She was a good sort of homely woman, not disinclined, now and then, to a little chat; and on the present occasion she seemed disposed to take the initiative.

Instead of removing the tray, she fidgetted a little with the tray-cloth, and, after clearing her throat, said, rather hesitatingly—

" Pray, sir, if I may be so bold as to ask, do you ever give lessons ?"

“Well, no,” said Mr. Antony, in surprise. “That is, I certainly did give a few lessons to a young lady once; but it is not in my line.”

“I humbly beg your pardon, sir. I hope no offence?”

“None at all, Mrs. Saffery.”

“Then, as you did give lessons to a young lady once, sir, maybe you might not quite object to do so again?”

“Well, I hardly know,” said Mr. Antony, rousing up at the thought of pounds, shillings, and pence, and yet not much relishing the way by which they were to be acquired. “Do you know any one in this neighbourhood in want of lessons?”

“Nessy, sir.”

“Nessy!” repeated he with surprise and aversion. “Oh, Mrs. Saffery! that would not suit me at all. I mean, it would not suit *you*. My terms would be too high.”

“We concluded, sir,” resumed Mrs. Saffery after a pause, “that your terms would be high. Whether they would be *too* high is another question.”

“What should you say to half-a-guinea an

hour, for instance ?" said Mr. Antony, thinking to startle her.

"Half-a-guinea an hour," said Mrs. Saffery, after another pause, "is a considerable sum, sir. There are many that couldn't pay it. Being so high, it would compel Nessy to have the fewer lessons. But then, sir, we should always have the privilege of saying that Nessy had had the best of teaching at half-a-guinea a lesson. It might be an advantage to her, sir, all her life."

This was such an unexpected argument, that Mr. Antony had not, for the moment, one word to say in reply. But his repugnance to teaching Nessy was undiminished.

"Mrs. Saffery," said he, rather haughtily, "you don't quite understand our relative positions. I am *not* a professed teacher; I feel as if I should be letting myself down somewhat by it—at least, by teaching such a very little girl as Nessy."

"Nessy's older than she looks," put in Mrs. Saffery.

"Yes, yes, I know ; but still, she's *very* young, and has had no previous instruction."

"I thought, sir, that might be an advantage."

"Well, perhaps it is so," he reluctantly admitted; "but why should you think it?"

"All the easier, sir—"

"Oh no, you're quite on the wrong tack," interrupted he. "It is merely that I should not have the faults of a bad teacher to correct, as well as her own."

"The mind of youth has been compared to a sheet of white paper," observed Mrs. Saffery; adding, with a view to improve the illustration, "on which you may draw either landscapes or figures."

"Ay; or carts and horses; or pigs and poultry."

"Then, sir," said Mrs. Saffery, after another and longer pause, "I'm afraid I am to understand you decline the proposal."

"Well—no," said poor Antony, as the question of ways and means rose up against him. "I don't like to disappoint you, Mrs. Saffery, but I really think you might employ your money better."

"Sir," said Mrs. Saffery, "*we* must be the best judges of that."

" But it really will seem to me like picking your pocket."

" Why should it, sir? We have a certain sum per annum to lay out on Nessy's teaching; and it may as well go into your pocket as any one else's."

" But an inferior and cheaper master would suit your purpose as well or better."

" Are the cheapest things, sir, always the best ?"

" No; but you really are taking me too much on trust. You don't know that my teaching will be worth the money."

" Oh, sir! those lovely things of yours!" said Mrs. Saffery, extending her hand towards his pictures, and gazing towards them in fond admiration.

Mr. Antony could not help smiling, and feeling mollified.

" You take a deal of persuading, sir," she added.

" Well, I do," said he, " because, you see, it's against my judgment, and against my inclination, too. For I don't hesitate to say, Mrs. Saffery, that I am not, in a general way, fond of teaching."

"Perhaps, sir, the young lady you mentioned as having taught was particularly troublesome."

"No, she was not," he said, hastily. "Well, Mrs. Saffery, since you will have it so, so let it be. But the lesson must be one hour long, and no longer."

"Suppose, sir, since you are so afraid of its being too long, we divide it, and say half an hour at a time for five and threepence. That would come easy."

"I don't think we could do much good in half an hour," said Mr. Antony. "However, we'll see. So, let Nessy come to me to-morrow morning at ten o'clock."

On this, Mrs. Saffery was voluble in thanks, and at length she carried out the supper-tray, leaving him hardly conscious whether he were annoyed or pleased. It is certain he was not in a very good humour that night; and after spending half an hour very discontentedly, he carried himself and his discontent to bed.

Next morning, true to the hour, Nessy appeared in her shabby-genteel black silk frock, staid and prim as usual, but immensely happy, though rather embarrassed.

"Well, Nessy, here you are," began Mr. Antony, looking up. Now, then, for it. Let us see what we shall see. Can you use a piece of chalk?"

"I dare say I can, sir."

"Humph! Can you cut it?"

"Yes, sir."

"Well, now, here's a piece of cartridge-paper, and here's a piece of chalk. Draw some lines like these."

"Oh!" said Nessy, in blank dismay, "*that's* not what I was to learn!"

"Not what you were to learn? Why, what were you to learn?"

"To paint in oils."

"My good girl, if you were going to build a house, should you begin with the chimney-pot?"

"No," said Nessy, resentfully, and losing all her fear of him under the burning sense of indignity at being called a good girl.

"Well, that would be just like beginning to paint before you can draw."

"But I *can* draw, and I don't want to draw," she answered, impetuously. "I want to paint, and it is for painting only that my mamma is willing to give so much money."

"Whew! Good morning, Nessy."

Her throat swelled. "I don't call *you* Leonard, sir!"

"I stand corrected, Miss Saffery. Good morning, miss. Our engagement, if you please, is ended." And he sat down, and began to write a letter.

Nessy stood still, and silently cried. Presently he looked up.

"Well, Miss Saffery, I must say this is not very polite."

"I hope you'll forgive me, sir."

"No, I don't think I shall."

Tears flowed afresh. The letter was continued.

"Well, Miss Saffery, I really am surprised. I thought this room was my own for the time being."

"Sir, I am going," said Nessy, in smothered accents; yet still she stayed. A long pause.

"Well, Miss Saffery?"

She walked a step or two towards him.

"Oh, what an opportunity to lose! Sir, *will* you teach me?"

He burst into a roar of laughter. She looked amazed and scandalized.

"Were you laughing at me all the while?" said she.

"No, certainly not," said Mr. Antony; "but I never knew such a tragi-comedy. O Nessy! —Miss Saffery, I mean—"

"You may call me Nessy, sir, if you like."

"A thousand thanks for so inestimable a privilege. Well, Nessy, *are* you going to be a baby or a sensible girl?"

"A sensible girl—if I can, sir."

"Very well; then now for it. You know, if *you* are going to teach *me*, our positions are reversed. If I am going to teach you, you must mind what I say."

"Yes, sir."

Here Mrs. Saffery looked in, anxiously.

"I hope Nessy is getting on pretty well, sir?"

"Oh, swimmingly!"

"Be a good girl, Nessy."

(Exit Mrs. Saffery.)

"My mamma would be so disappointed," said Nessy, timidly, "if she thought I did not give satisfaction."

"Ah! it's a difficult thing to satisfy *me*," said Mr. Antony, with a sort of groan or grunt, accompanied by a terrific shake of the head. "Here, suppose you and I look over this portfolio of pictures together."

Nessy was silently transported.

"There! what do you call that?"

"That's a man."

"Clever girl! Yes; and that's a woman."

"Not a very pretty one," said Nessy.

"*Not* pretty?" and he looked daggers. "Pray, Miss Saffery, what is the matter with her?"

"Her nose is too straight."

"Why, that's a Grecian nose. A Grecian nose is beautiful!"

Nessy was silenced; but she did not think her a pretty lady.

"She has a pretty name," observed she, finding Mr. Antony continued to look at the head, and wishing to conciliate. "Is her name Rosabel?"

"It is, and yet it is not," said he oracularly; and he turned another drawing over it.

"There. What's that?"

"An angel."

"Is the angel's dress in straight lines?"

"No, wavy."

"That wavy line is the line of beauty. It is elegant, graceful. Straight, angular forms are ungraceful. Wavy lines are beautiful."

"I thought you said just now that straight noses were beautiful," said Nessy.

"Do you prefer crooked ones?" said he. "There; go and draw me some wavy figures on that cartridge paper."

"What sort of figures, sir?"

"Any sort you like, so that they abound in the line of beauty (waving his hand in the air)—fairies, angels, zephyrs."

She sat down to obey this vague direction as well as she could, and drew very quietly and patiently for nearly a quarter of an hour. Mr. Antony stood at his easel the while, and began filling in a background.

"Well," said he at length, "let me see how you are getting on. Come, this is famous. Here is the line of beauty and no mistake. Double s's running into one another as they do in the Lord Mayor's gold collar."

She drew a deep breath.

"Are you tired?"

"A little."

"Well, your half-hour is almost up."

She looked at him with timid entreaty.

"Might not I paint, just for five minutes, sir?"

"Well, yes, if you like. I suppose nothing else will make you happy."

He put the brush and palette into her hands. She held them awkwardly, afraid of dropping them.

"What am I to do?"

"Here's a millboard that will be none the worse for a coat of paint. You may fill in a plain background all over it."

"What! all over that beautiful picture?"

"The picture is not beautiful, and if you don't cover it over, I shall."

"Oh, then I will!" cried Nessy. "Which colour, sir?"

"Mix them all together into a sort of sky-blue scarlet."

She knew he was laughing at her, but she did not mind. It was so delightful to handle the palette-knife! When she had mixed all the colours together, she found they made a dirty drab.

"Is that sky-blue scarlet, sir?"

"Well, it will do for it. Now take the

largest brush. *Laissez-aller.* Don't crumple up your fingers as if they were tied together with a piece of string. Don't niggle-naggle. Firmer, firmer. That's better. That's well."

After working away for some time with evident enjoyment, she looked up at him with a smile, and said—

"At any rate, it teaches me the use of the brush."

Mr. Antony's conscience smote him for letting her waste her time so; but, in fact, she was not wasting it.

"Now hatch it," said he, taking the brush from her and showing her what he meant. "That's right. Come, you'll beat Apelles some day."

"Or Nicholas Poussin," observed Nessy, smiling.

"Ay, you know more about him."

"There's something about Apelles though, sir, in Butler's ' Globes.' "

"Ah, that's a book of universal information. Have you been through all the problems ? "

"No, sir."

Here Mrs. Saffery looked in with a smile and said—

"Nessy, the time's up."

"Oh!" said Nessy, with a start, "how sorry I am!"

"Stay, you may as well just cover the mill-board," said Mr. Antony, "or I shall have to do so myself. Another five minutes will finish it."

"There's no more paint, sir."

"No? Then we must have a little more. Squeeze it out of these little tubes. Not too hard, or you'll burst them, and spoil your frock. I advise you not to paint in a silk frock in future."

"It is such an honour to paint at all, that I think I ought to wear my best," said Nessy.

"Things that are inappropriate are not the best. Some day you'll upset the palette on your frock, and then who will you have to thank? Wilful waste brings woful want. That's why I didn't bring my best hat into the country."

"Did not you, sir?" said Nessy, in surprise, which made him laugh.

"There, now you've done it! What a splendid achievement!"

"Good morning, sir. Thank you."

"You had better take that chalk and cartridge paper with you, and draw some more angels."

"Do you believe in angels, sir?"

"Believe in them? Yes, to be sure! and in zephyrs and fairies, and all such things. Do you think I'm a Sadducee? Here, Nessy, just stop while I show you one thing."

She hesitated, looked wistful, but went towards the door.

"No, sir, my lesson's over. I must not use any more of your time."

And the door closed after her.

"A conscientious little monkey," muttered Mr. Antony.

CHAPTER V.

PYRRHUS.

On the first Sunday of Mr. Antony's stay at the post-office, Mrs. Saffery had said to her husband at dinner-time—

"Where did Mr. Antony sit in church this morning?"

"I don't think he sat anywhere," said Mr. Saffery. "I don't believe he was in church."

"No, I don't think he was," said Nessy.

"That's abominable," said Mrs. Saffery. "I've no notion of young men being infidels and heretics; let them be the finest young gentlemen ever born. I shall tell him a bit of my mind, if I find it's the case."

"Oh, mother, don't," said Nessy, hastily.

"But indeed I shall, though," said Mrs. Saffery. "Many a man's soul has been lost through the false shame of his neighbours."

"False nonsense, my dear," said Mr. Saffery.

"You shouldn't judge folks so hastily. Mr. Antony may have been in church after all, or have had some good reason for staying away. He may not have had a hymn-book."

"That's true," said Mrs. Saffery, "though he might have asked for one, and that was a poor reason for keeping from church. However, he shall not have that objection to make this afternoon."

So when the church bell began to go, she tapped at her lodger's door, and on his saying, "Come in," she entered with a bland smile, and found him lounging in the American chair, reading the Artist's World.

"Oh, sir, our afternoon service begins at three," said she, in carefully modulated tones ; "and though the church is rather full of a morning, there's always plenty of room in the afternoons. I thought you might be glad of one of the hymn-books we use—it's the collection authorized by the Bishop of London, and published by Routledge, price fourpence." Saying which, she laid the little book on the table.

"Thank you," drily said Mr. Antony, resuming his reading in a posture of more complete ease.

Mrs. Saffery was a good deal excited. "I don't believe," said she, returning to her husband, "that he has any more idea of stirring than that table."

"Well, my dear, it's no business of ours," said the placid Mr. Saffery.

"Strictly speaking, it may not be; but I can't see a fine young man going to wrack and ruin without feeling pained. It's not in my nature. Catch me remembering to let him have the next Artist's World till Monday morning!"

"Why, if you don't give it him, he'll only ask for it; and if he don't get it, he'll only read something else," said Mr. Saffery.

"Then I hope it will be something awakening," said Mrs. Saffery.

Nessy had been alarmed and pained by this little dialogue, and she felt uncomfortable whenever the subject of Mr. Antony's faith and practice occurred to her. *Now* she seemed to have found the solution of the enigma, so at dinner she cheerfully said, "Mamma, I know why Mr. Antony does not go to church; it's because he has not brought his best hat."

"Nonsense!" said Mrs. Saffery, in disgust;

"he didn't expect you to believe that, did he? His hat is good enough, and besides, he would not wear it in church."

This had not occurred to Nessy. "At any rate," said she, in a lower voice, "he believes in angels, and he says he is not a Sadducee."

"What a very odd remark," said her mother. "No, nor a Pharisee, neither, of course. Why, the Pharisees and Sadducees were Jews; and he isn't a Jew, even if he is not a Christian. I tell you what, Nessy. Mr. Antony is a good deal cleverer than you or I, whatever his principles may be, and I don't pay him to teach you religion, but painting; so you must let alone these kind of subjects, or I shall stop short your lessons. Your business is to paint, not to talk."

This was a check to poor Nessy, who feared losing her lessons more than anything.

"Now, here's a stupid thing for somebody to go and do," said Michael Saffery, beginning to stamp the letters. "Here's somebody been and posted a letter without ever a direction on it. Where is it to go to, I wonder?"

"To the dead-letter office, of course," said his wife; "but, dear me, Michael, let us try to

make out who can have put it in.   Is there a
seal upon it ? "

" Yes, with Q. P."

" Why, that's Quintillia Prosser !   Of course
you know Mrs. Prosser's name is Quintillia, because she signs it to her money-orders."

" Well, but of course I don't know who Mrs.
Prosser meant to direct this letter to."

" No, but Nessy can take it to her and get
her to direct it.   One would not wish to dis-
oblige Mrs. Prosser.   Put on your bonnet,
Nessy, this minute, and run off with it."

Nessy was just then about some little affair
or other that she particularly disliked being
interrupted in.   However, she put it aside and
dressed herself for the walk.   It was a pleasant
afternoon, and the air was very fresh and sweet
as she crossed the common on the skirts of
which was Mrs. Prosser's cottage.   It stood a
little below the turfy, undulating waste, so that
you only saw the brown tiled roof till you
came close upon the white palings ; and then a
steep little pebbled path took you down to the
porch, which, in heavy rains, was apt to be
under water.   Nessy was always fond of this
place, though she could not tell why.   It was

like two or three small cottages converted into one ; and hardly two rooms in it were on the same level.

Mrs. Prosser was one of those very clever people who sometimes do very stupid things. She had been in great haste, she said, which must have occasioned the oversight, and she was very much obliged to Mr. Saffery for sending back the letter, and to Nessy for bringing it. She hoped she had not minded the walk. Oh, no, Nessy said, she liked it very much. Altogether, it was a bright, pleasant little interview, and Nessy was glad Mrs. Prosser had forgotten to direct the letter.

She walked home more at her leisure— *daunering*, as the Scotch say, and pausing here and there to look about her and enjoy the pleasant air. A river, winding through the lower ground, lost itself in a tangled thicket ; some anglers were crossing it in a punt ; on the other bank were one or two of their party hallooing and beckoning. All at once Nessy was reminded of the description of Poussin's picture, " The Saving of Pyrrhus." She had a great desire—" ambition," her mother would have called it—to produce a sketch, and here was a subject ! She hastily pulled out a crumpled piece of paper and the stump of a pencil, and rudely scrawled the scene, writing "trees " and " grass " at certain points of it.

That evening, when her day's work was done, Nessy busied herself by making what artists would call a finished study of this piece. First, she drew it out on a slate ; after several corrections of the original sketch, she copied it on the cartridge paper ; taking care to introduce the withies, the ashes, the poplars, the sedges, the water, the boat, and the steep, broken foreground. All this, of course, was very rudely portrayed. Then she put in the figures, which were still worse executed, but in lively action. Costume, of course, of no particular period.

As Mr. Antony's stay was expected to be short, it had been arranged that Nessy should take four half-lessons a week, viz., on Tuesday, Wednesday, Thursday, and Friday. Saturday and Monday were busy days, when Nessy was expected to attend to certain light tasks in the way of dusting and cleaning, getting up fine linen, gathering fruit and vegetables, shelling peas, stringing and slitting French beans, topping and tailing gooseberries, &c.; employments that her mother averred no lady need think scorn of. At all events, Nessy liked them very well, and never thought of despising them ; so that, on the whole, her time passed as happily as a little girl's time could.

When she tapped at Mr. Antony's door, in readiness for her second lesson, he called out, "Come in," in his usual cheerful manner.

"Stop a bit," said he, without looking up, as she entered, "I want just to finish what I'm about before I attend to you."

"Yes, sir ;" and she stood a few paces behind him, watching him with deep interest. He was painting a little landscape with figures.

"Now then," said he, at last, laying down palette and brushes, and turning round upon her. "I suppose you've a basketful of angels? Hallo ! what's this ?"

"The saving of Pyrrhus, sir."

"The *what* ?"

In a much lower voice, she repeated, "The saving of Pyrrhus."

"Who's Pyrrhus ?"

Nessy did not know. She believed he was a prince or king, or something of that sort.

"King of what?"

She could not tell.

"Well, this is the funniest thing I *ever* heard of. To draw a picture of you don't know what and cannot tell ! Why, Nessy," after a long pause, during which she felt penetrated with shame, "you don't know how well, in some respects, you've done this !"

She gave a great start.

"Here's *genius !* But you don't know what that is, neither. Where did you get this background ? "

"Oh, sir," said Nessy, colouring crimson, "you must not think it invention. I copied it."

"Oh ! From what ? "

"From Fairlee Common, as I crossed it yesterday."

"And the boat ? "

"The boat was there too, and some of the people."

"Men in Greek tunics ? "

"No, I took them from the picture-Bible, because I did not know how people dressed in Pyrrhus's time."

"Hum—combination. What on earth put Pyrrhus into your head ? "

"One of Poussin's pictures, sir. The description of it, I mean."

"Turn it up. I don't remember it."

Nessy speedily found the description, and showed it him. He read it very attentively, with a little frown on his brow, which made her doubtful whether he were pleased or the reverse.

"Humph," said he at last; "it is a queer thing to take hold of you. You've got it all in, one way or another, nurses, soldiers, and all. The figures, preposterous, of course. Still—" and a long pause ensued.

"Nessy," said he abruptly, at length, "you are but a little girl, whatever you may think, but I'm going to talk to you, for once, as if you were a woman." And he looked grave, almost stern. "I said, just now, you had genius. Have you the least idea what that means?"

Nessy blushed painfully, and said, "Yes, sir."

"Oh, you have, have you? What is it?"

After a pause, she said, "A person may know what a thing is, without knowing how to explain it."

"I won't admit that. Come, try at it."

"Genius makes you do at a thought—almost without thought—what others can't do with ever so much thinking."

"Not bad that. But you hardly improved it by adding 'almost without thought.' '*At a thought*,' was the thing. It don't come without thinking. And that one particular thought that hits the mark comes of many foregone and wistful thoughts, that seemed to have no particular end. They wrap themselves up, at last, into this bright thought that suddenly knocks the nail on the head!" And he rapped the table with his knuckles. "D'ye see?"

"Yes, sir."

Another pause.

"There are many people, Nessy, who never attain to that one bright thought—they go on hammering and hammering, this side and that side the nail, very close to it sometimes, *but never on the head*."

"No, sir."

"Those people," pursued Mr. Antony, frowning darkly, "when they see *you* hit the nail, cry, 'bless my soul, how was it *I* could not do that? That's just what I meant to do, and

was going to do, only you've done it first.'
Don't believe it! They would *never* have done
it!" And he shook his finger at her.

"No, sir."

"Just as if you knew anything about it,"
muttered he, after another pause. Nessy felt
aggrieved.

"Now," resumed he, "after what I've said
of genius, very likely you think those who have
it have won the battle. Quite a mistake. Because genius is a gift, that doesn't make it
self-sufficient. Because you've a nose, that
does not enable you to do without eyes and
mouth, does it?"

"No, sir."

"And what's the good of a mouth without
something to eat? No more good than genius
without workmanship! Genius is a capital
thing, Nessy, to start with; but it's no good
at all, you'd far better be without it, unless
you know how to use it. Now, at present you
don't know how to use yours. You know
absolutely nothing. And I don't see how you
are ever to learn much. And I don't see what
good it would be to you to learn much."

"Oh, sir!" And Nessy looked miserably

disappointed. "I thought," faltered she, "it was always good for us to improve our minds."

"If we *do* improve them," said Mr. Antony. "But we are not improved by what takes us out of our own sphere."

"I thought all that was settled, sir, between you and my mamma. Surely we need not go all over it again?"

"Well, no. It has been decided that I am to give you a little smattering of drawing, and it will be but a little smattering, Nessy. You must not plume yourself on having had a few lessons, and fancy they have taught you everything; for, at best, they can but teach you very little. A man cannot learn to make a pianoforte at the first trial; no more can you learn to paint. It requires a long apprenticeship. And if it was needful for you to undergo that apprenticeship, you have a very fair capital of genius to start with. But happily for you, it's not needful. I say happily, because you would find it very hard and very ill-rewarded work. So many others are in the field, that even when you deserve it, you can't always get on."

She sighed.

"As for this sketch, I advise you to put it in the fire."

"Oh, sir!"

"Yes, put it in the fire, I say; there's no real value in it; though, considering the circumstances, it is a curiosity. Artists would only laugh at it."

Oh, surprise! Mrs. Saffery, opening the door, said, "Nessy! your time's up." And Nessy had done nothing.

CHAPTER VI.

A VISITOR.

"I MUST say, sir," said Mrs. Saffery, presently returning to the parlour, where Mr. Antony was sitting in a thoughtful posture—"I must say, sir," said she in an accusatory tone, "that I didn't expect Nessy to be a wasting of her time as I find she's been a doing this morning. You must have the kindness, sir, to keep her to it a little more strictly, if you please."

"It was my fault, Mrs. Saffery; I was talking to her."

"Well then, sir, if I may say so without offence, we are not rich enough people for you to be talking to her at five-and-threepence the half-hour."

"Of course not. I did not consider the lesson begun. Send her back; she shall have it now."

"No, sir, she has one of her bad headaches.

Nessy's a curious child, she doesn't bear too much thinking; and it was partly because her father and I did not like to see her so much at her books, that we wished her to paint, as we noticed, sir, that you always stood at your easel, and that your sketching took you so much into the open air."

"That's true; but you are mistaken, Mrs. Saffery, if you suppose that painting does not require thinking. It requires constant thought of the closest kind; a really good painter has his art always in his head—always is taking notice of happy effects in light and shade, bits of drapery, &c. For instance, there's a capital fold at this instant in your apron, Mrs. Saffery; don't move, for your life! I'll jot it down in a moment. I beg your pardon."

Poor Mrs. Saffery stood transfixed, like the Lady in Comus, for full five minutes, wishing the artist at Jericho.

"There!" said he, presently, "that bell-shaped fold was too good to lose. Well, Mrs. Saffery, you see I had a great deal to explain to your little girl this morning. . She fancies, and so do you, that one may be an artist at a jump; at any rate, in five or six lessons. My good lady, do you think you could teach me to make a gooseberry-pie in five or six lessons?"

"Well, sir," said Mrs. Saffery, beginning to smile, "I'm afraid your crust might be heavy. You see, that's woman's work."

"Oh, pardon me! we have plenty of French pastrycooks, and Scotchmen, and Italians too."

"Well, sir, you see they're taught."

"That's the very thing," said he, quickly. "They have a seven years' apprenticeship. And do you think it easier to paint a picture than to make a pie?"

"Well, sir, many ladies paint very prettily."

Mr. Antony shrugged his shoulders. "They had better stick to their bead-work and button-holes," said he. "At least, that's my mind."

"It will never be theirs, sir."

"No, I am afraid not."

"Then, since that's the case, sir, why should not Nessy paint like the rest? Just in a lady's way, you know, sir."

"Well," said he, "the fact is, Nessy might do better than nine ladies out of ten, if she were regularly put to it."

"Would not it be worth while, then, sir,"

said Mrs. Saffery, brightening, "to put her regularly to it?"

"To what end? In the first place, you would not like the means. They would be expensive, and take her quite away from her usual work—set her above it."

"That would be bad, certainly," said Mrs. Saffery.

"Yes, and even supposing her health could bear the training, which I very much doubt, if half an hour's quiet talking, such as you and I are having now, gives her a nervous headache."

"Oh, sir, I doubt it too!"

"Very well; but even supposing her health to bear it, and supposing her to become as good an artist as I am, for instance—which indeed, Mrs. Saffery, vanity apart, is a very wide supposition—what has she attained *then*? —what have I? Have *I* made my fortune, or secured a lasting fame? is my name even familiar to my countrymen?"

He shook his head. "They hang my pictures—not in the silver teapot row or the silver milk-jug row; no, nor yet even in the dead-game row!—but at the very top or else at the very bottom."

" Is it possible, sir!" said Mrs. Saffery, "that there can exist such bribery and corruption?"

He could not help laughing a little. "Not in reality, perhaps," said he, "but people will consider their own friends first, and we, the overlooked, are apt to attribute all our slights to envy and malice."

"Ah, that's human nature, sir ; but *you*—that *you* should be overlooked!"

" Wonderful, isn't it? But, you see, I am but young yet, and have time to make my way. Perhaps at sixty I may have made my fame."

" I hope so, sir."

" Meanwhile, you see, I paint to live, instead of living to paint. And the upshot of it is, Mrs. Saffery, that you may be very glad your little girl is not a little boy, with his way to make in the world."

" Yes, sir, I am very thankful Nessy is provided for."

" Send her out to pick gooseberries, since her head aches with thinking too much ; and let her come to me to-morrow."

When Nessy came to him the following day, he said, very calmly—

" Well, now we will propose to ourselves

some easy task that shall not be too much for our nerves. I think it will be best for you not to aim at the highflying school, severe history, and so forth : leave Pyrrhus, Pericles, and all the rest of them, to take care of themselves, and stick to little rustic pieces."

" Yes, sir."

" By-the-way, let me have another look at that grand performance of yours."

" Oh, sir ! I burned it."

" Burned it ? "

" You told me to do so," said Nessy, her lip quivering.

" But I did not think you would."

" I wish I had known that, I'm sure, for I should have liked very much to keep it."

" Well, I am sorry I told you so, since it gave you so much pain. However, I give you credit for it; and it really is a good thing to have cleared it away, for you could have made nothing of it."

" It would have been pleasant to look at sometimes."

From this time, Mr. Antony gave Nessy his best attention, both in drawing and painting; so that in a fortnight, it was surprising how much progress she had made. In fact, her mind was at work all day long, and even in her dreams; so that Mrs. Saffery, fearing she would be ill, invented errands that continually sent her into the open air.

One day, when Nessy returned from one of these excursions, her mother was dismissing a tall, pale, thin old man, who seemed to have been seeking relief without getting any. Deeply sighing as he turned away, he said—

"I think I'll go into the House. There I shall, at any rate, have plenty of victuals, and a roof over my head; but somehow I don't think I can stand being shut up, for I've been in the open air all my life, and I did hope that nothing but death would part my old mistress and me."

Mr. Antony, as he passed through the shop, was struck by the unaffected expression of pity on Nessy's face. She was feeling in her empty pocket.

"Hallo, old man," said he, "what's the matter with you?"

"Nothing, sir," said the old man, "but want."

"Do you want to have your likeness taken?"

"You're a merry young gentleman, sir. I wish I wanted nothing more than I want that."

"Well, but *I* want to take it, if you don't, which comes to the same thing. Your withered cheek, and tresses grey, seem to have known a better day. Step in here, my old friend; I'll hit you off in ten minutes, and then give you a shilling."

The old man, in surprise and joy, followed him into the parlour, saying, "You may hit me as much as you like, sir, if you don't hit too hard."

"Is not that nice, mother?" said Nessy, gladly.

"Yes, very nice," said Mrs. Saffery. "And, now I think of it, there's a bit of cold hashed mutton, not enough for a dinner, but quite enough for a relish, which you may put into the oven for him if you like, and give him when he comes out."

"Oh, thank you!"

When the old man, who had enjoyed a good chat with Mr. Antony during the sitting, came out with the shilling in his pocket and a smile on his face, Nessy met him with the plate of warm food and a piece of bread.

"Do you mean this is for me?" said he, in a glow of pleasure, as she presented it to him. "Well, this *is* a bright day for me, that I thought was going to be so dark. For what I am going to receive, may the Lord make me truly thankful!"

"You may come again to-morrow," said Mr. Antony.

"Thank'e, sir! thank'e!"

Nessy had set him a little table, with a knife and fork, and he despatched his little meal so like a famished man that she thought it a painful pleasure to watch him. The thought suddenly was borne in upon her—

"Surely, there can be no happiness equal to that of giving food to the hungry!"

Day followed day. Mr. Antony had been nearly a month at the post-office, when he told Mrs. Saffery, to her great regret, that he was going to return home at the end of the week. This was a sad blow to Nessy, but she had known it must fall. Notwithstanding his having been mischievous enough to dismay Mrs. Saffery by saying to her one Sunday, "Cannot Nessy and I have a little painting this morning?" he really had gone punctually to church, though occasionally in some distant village ; spending the interim between the services in the open air.

On the morning of his last day, as Nessy was reluctantly leaving the room at the end of her last lesson, the parlour door suddenly opened, and, instead of Mrs. Saffery, there appeared a vision of delight in the person of a very bright, blooming young lady, who looked brimful of mirth and sure of a welcome.

"Hallo, Edith ! how are you, old girl ?"

She burst out laughing, and they kissed one another. Nessy vanished.

"Why, how glad I am to see you ? Why did not you come before ?"

"Why did you never ask me, Mr. Leo ?"

"I did !"

"No, not once ! You said you were sorry I could not come."

"Because I thought you would not. And, besides, I knew that there is not a corner in this house in which to put you."

"That's a valid argument ; however, you might have asked me to come for the day, as I've come now."

"And you might have come for the day without asking, as you have come now !"

On which they joined again in a merry laugh.

"I'm very glad you *are* come," said he, taking her hand. "How well you are looking!"

"Oh, no; the paint has half poisoned me."

"Why did not you stay with Miss Hill?"

"She was so tedious. I preferred the paint."

"Was not that tedious too?"

"Well, they have been very slow about it, but it looks so nice now! And we have clean blinds and clean curtains and—"

"And I hope Martha has a clean face."

Edith laughed and said, "It is always clean in the afternoon. You must not expect too much of her in the morning."

"What! not to wash her face when she gets up?"

"Oh dear, no, Leonard! Only think, Mrs. Gregory rings her up at five, and she dresses by candlelight."

"Not at this time of year. She puts on her clothes with a pitchfork, does not she?"

"If you knew what it is to be a lodging-house servant, you would not be so hard on poor Martha."

"I hope I should always begin by washing my face."

"Well, but what have you been doing? Falling in love with another pupil?"

"How can you talk such rubbish; my pupil went out as you came in."

"That plain little girl?" said Edith, raising her eyebrows.

"Hush! walls have ears: and these walls are thin. She's a clever little body. Besides, what nonsense you were talking just now of 'another' pupil! Just as if a man could care for two at once. By-the-bye, have you seen Rosabel lately?"

"Yes, I have."

"Tell me all about it," said he, eagerly.

"There's not much to tell. I met her and her father coming along the square. They both saw me, but he pretended not to do so. She would have stopped, but he pulled her on: so she gave me this kind of look—as much as to say 'you see how it is!'"

"Brute!"

"Well, I don't think it's any good for you to mind it, or to think much about her, for I fear nothing can come of it."

"Just as if I could help it!"

"Every man ought to be able to govern his own mind."

Mr. Antony sighed like a furnace.

"You don't know what my feelings are," said he.

"Oh yes, I do, pretty well. But, Leo, we can talk about this at home. What shall we do here? Show me your sketches. I see you have a pretty little thing on the easel—just such as I told you to paint."

"Painted to order, then."

"This will be sure to sell. And here is a nice study of an old beggar; 'Pity the sorrows of a poor old man,' will be just the motto for it."

"By-the-bye, Edith, you must be hungry. What will you have? Marmalade, anchovy paste, eggs and bacon, bread and butter, or what?"

"Nothing before dinner, thank you. I had a bun as I came along."

"Ah, I must think about dinner. If you had given me notice, we might have had salmon and lobster-sauce, ham and chicken, rhubarb tart and custard."

"Only, as I did not, we must have two

mutton-chops and two potatoes! Well, it will not be the first time. But I don't care about dinner, I want to take a long walk first."

"With all my heart. Where shall we go?"

"Oh, I must put myself under your guidance."

"Suppose we go to the Dulwich gallery. Do you mind stretching out three or four miles?"

"Not in the least. I am as fresh as a lark, and shall enjoy it of all things."

"Suppose we take little Miss Saffery with us."

"Oh, no! that would spoil sport. Suppose we take some bread and butter with us, and have our mutton-chops at tea. Then we shall be independent."

"Yes, that's well thought of. Perhaps Mrs. Saffery will contrive us some sandwiches out of something or nothing, and let us have some biscuits."

He rang the bell. Nessy answered it.

"Nessy, my sister and I are going to walk over to the Dulwich gallery, and we shall not want our dinner till tea-time; then we will have them both together. But it is a long walk, and ladies are apt to get hungry, so that if Mrs.

Saffery could by any possibility invent a few sandwiches for us, we should be infinitely obliged. And do you think, Nessy, we could have a few biscuits ? "

" Oh, yes ! " said Nessy, with alacrity, " I'll go for them myself, and lend you a pretty little basket. It will hold the sandwiches besides, and I'm sure mamma can cut some slices off the Bath chop."

Her blue eyes seemed to smile as she spoke ; and, after bestowing an admiring look on Edith, she retired, on hospitable thoughts intent.

" She seems a nice little thing," said Edith. " Suppose we revise our sentence, and take her, if you think she would care to go."

" Let her get the biscuits first," said Mr. Antony. " One thing at a time will last the longer."

When Nessy came in with her basket, she was almost out of her mind with joy at the invitation that awaited her. She had been thinking how Mr. Antony and his sister were going to enjoy themselves, and how delightful it would be to be either of them ; and now, to be asked to make a third !

> " O, che gioia ! che contento !
> Di picer mi balza il cor ! "

CHAPTER VII.

NESSY ENCHANTED.

"It was so kind of you to let me come," said Nessy, shyly, to Edith as they started.

"Kindness is its own reward then," said Edith laughing, "since you have undertaken to carry the basket."

It will suffice to say of the walk in general terms, that it was delightful. It led them across the country, through out-of-the-way places, and now and then Mr. Antony caused a halt, that he might sketch. On the confines of an old deserted house, that looked gloomy, windy, and full of ghosts, they came to a gap in some mossy park-palings, within which was a sylvan brake that Edith pronounced the very spot for their sandwiches. A felled tree afforded them an excellent seat; and Nessy, with some self-importance; first unfolded a tray napkin at the top of her basket, and spread it for a tablecloth; then placed on it a very respectable packet of sandwiches, three hard-boiled eggs, and a little paper of biscuits. Mr. Antony declared that one of the eggs was much larger than the others, and insisted they should draw lots for it with dandelion-stalks. And his sense of equity was so exact that he made Nessy count the sandwiches into three allotments, and distribute them equally. He said they wanted nothing but strawberries and cream.

"There must always be a want," said Edith. "The best way is to be content with what we have.

> " What though from fortune's lavish bounty,
>   No mighty treasures we possess,
>   We'll find within our pittance plenty,
>   And be content without excess."

"If we are all going to say a hymn, I'll repeat 'The Little Busy Bee,'" said Mr. Antony.

"I'll give you my last sandwich if you can say two verses without missing a word."

He did so, and had the sandwich.

"Now then, Miss Saffery, I call upon you."

"Oh, no!" said Nessy, hastily; "I can't say anything."

"Not even the multiplication table?"

She smiled and said she did not think he would care to hear that.

"Let us start some improving subject, however. Who is the greatest living painter?"

"Mr. Antony."

"There, Leonard! You are satisfied, I hope. What a pretty spot this is; it is like one of Ruysdael's pictures."

"No, it is not. You'll see some of his pictures presently."

"Well, but they are not all alike. Miss Hill told me a curious fact, Leo, about Wordsworth."

"What was it?"

"His eyes used to get very much inflamed, particularly when he was composing; but the inflammation was very much subdued by his looking at pictures. They amused his mind, which, no longer fretting at his ailment, allowed his eyes to get well."

"Nothing like leather," said Mr. Antony, which seemed to Nessy an irrelevant remark.

"I should think the fairies danced here on moonlight nights," continued Edith.

"To what music?"

"'The pipe of Pan, to shepherds crouched in the shadow of Menalian pines.'"

"If I had a fiddle, I would play while you and Miss Saffery danced."

"Or you might dance to your own playing," said Edith, laughing as if the idea tickled her fancy.

"Edith, you are weak, or you could not laugh at such nonsense. Come, we had better go forward."

Laughing and talking, they soon found themselves within the precincts of the secluded college.

"What shall we do with the basket and sketchbook?" said Edith. "Shall we leave them under the hedge?"

"No, put them in that empty cart."

"Suppose the cart should go away."

"There is no horse in it."

"Suppose somebody should steal them."

"Not a creature is near."

So they put the basket, the book, and an umbrella into the cart, and then entered the college. The gallery-keeper, looking at Nessy, said,

"We don't admit children under twelve."

"I'm thirteen," cried Nessy.

"This lady is thirteen," said Mr. Antony; "her birthday was on the 25th of March—"

("No, the first of August!")

"Oh, yes! the first of August. What a memory I have! She is above the age; you have done her gross injustice."

The keeper smiled and let her pass. So they entered the suite of three rooms, in which there was not another living creature.

"Come, this is nice!" said Edith. "We have the gallery all to ourselves. You soon put down the keeper."

"I saw it was necessary to take a firm tone," said Mr. Antony, with one of his awful looks.

"Taking a firm tone means bullying, does not it?"

"Bullying is not a lady's word."

"Is it a gentleman's deed?"

"Only in politics now and then."

"Bringing a barbarous nation to reason, for instance?"

"Just so. Look at this Wouvermanns."

"How charming. The man on the bank seems spying at that ship in the offing. How unaffectedly earnest all the figures are, in whatever they are engaged!"

"Good distance."

"Very."

"What is Miss Saffery looking at? A lady playing on a keyed instrument. You don't call that a good picture, Nessy?"

"I think it a pretty picture," said Nessy, continuing to look at it.

"Yes, so do I," said Edith. "I can almost hear the jingling wires. She is playing something of Sebastian Bach's."

"Come here, and I will show you something better."

"Oh, please let me go on regularly," implored Nessy.

"I obey commands. Now you are at the lady buying dead game of an old man. You like that, I suppose."

"Yes, I do. How nicely her satin dress is done!"

"Ah!—" drawing in his breath with a hissing sound.

"Is it not?"

"Yes, but it is not high art."

"Who said it was?" interposed Edith. "There is one glory of the sun, and one glory of the moon. Leo, what a capital Teniers that is! Teniers himself, and his wife, with foot-boy at their heels, sauntering out on a showery afternoon. How well the rain-clouds are done!"

"'There are so many of them.'"

"Oh! quoting my letter! That pricked you, did it?"

"Of course."

"But I don't think any one could have said so of *these* rain-clouds."

"No one but a gaby."

"You see, Leonard, this picture is so obviously original."

"Do you mean to say mine is not, Miss Edith?"

"Not like this."

"Granted."

Nessy was now looking at a hunting party. A man was taking a stone or thorn out of a mule's foot. The animal's pain was so naturally expressed, that it gave some pain to witness it.

"'Rubens' Mother!'" exclaimed Mr. Antony, with a burst of admiration. "Glorious!"

"That's a very nice old lady," said Nessy.

"Nice! what an unworthy expression!"

"What *should* I have said?"

"'Glorious,' of course," said Edith.

The brother and sister went into the details of the painting in a manner that Nessy liked to hear, though she could not entirely understand. Mr. Antony retreated a few paces, and looked up.

"Guercino's St. Cecilia," said he. "She plays other guess music than the lady on the keyed instrument."

"That charming Moorish girl with her lapful of flowers!" said Edith. "One of Murillo's prettiest domestic studies."

"Yes; but she has no ideal beauty. None of his women have."

Nessy was living quite in a world of her own, while she looked at the Meeting of Jacob and Rachel.

"Look here, Nessy!" said Mr. Antony, suddenly. "Here is David with the head of Goliath. Do you like it?"

"No," she said with aversion.

"No! Why, this is by your famous Poussin."

"Oh, *is* it?" cried she, surprised and disappointed.

"Yes. Does it not equal what you expected of him?"

"Oh, no! David has red hair."

"Nay, that's no great matter. Perhaps David's hair was red."

"No, he was a Jew. Jews are dark, with black hair."

"He consulted the general tone of his picture, which is red."

"Too red," said Edith. "He neglected Ephraim Holding's advice—'Don't put too much red in your brush.'"

"The manner is dry," said Mr. Antony, after a close survey; "but the picture has all his peculiar excellences—learning, propriety, dignity. The drawing is good; so is the expression."

"I think I might learn to like it better in time," said Nessy, who was reluctant to give up Poussin at first sight. "But there are many prettier pictures here."

"If you were told you might have four, which should they be?"

She looked full of thought, pressing her hands tightly together; and then said, "The Boy Eating the Cheese-cake, Jacob and Rachel, the Mule with the Hurt Foot, and the Lady Playing on the Harpsichord."

"Not bad, Nessy, though you might have chosen better than the last."

"Looking at that lady took away my head-ache."

"Indeed? Well, if she had such sedative power, you have wisdom in your choice."

"I," said Edith, "would have St. Cecilia, Murillo's Assumption of the Virgin, the Scene on the Sea-shore, and the Conflagration of a Town by Night."

"Oh, what bathos!"

"No; there is poetry in it."

"Which, of course, an authoress thinks more of than painting."

"Are you an authoress?" said Nessy, in surprise.

Edith smiled, but did not say whether or no. She stood much higher, however, in Nessy's estimation, from that moment.

"Mr. Antony has not told us," she presently observed, "which his four pictures would be."

"I think I would have Guido's St. John, Rubens' Mother, Rembrandt's Jacob's Dream, and one of the Cuyps."

"I don't much care for the Rembrandt," said Edith. "Jacob is so badly drawn."

"But the ladder is so wonderful. Come, let us sit down. Miss Saffery, do you see that door?"

"Yes."

"Suppose you go and open it, and look in."

"Oh dear," cried Nessy, "I could not take such a liberty!"

"I will give you sixpence if you will."

"Indeed I don't want sixpence! It would be so odd! The keeper might be there."

"I am sure he is not."

"Perhaps," cried Nessy, "there is some trick. I have heard my mamma say, that when she was a little girl, she was taken to the Painted Hall at Greenwich, and an old pensioner gave her a key, and said, 'If you will go and unlock that door, it will let you into Queen Anne's garden.' When she went close up to it, she found it was only painted—keyhole and all! There was no real door. My mamma said she could never help thinking that if there *had* been a door, it would have opened into a beautiful garden, full of terraces and fountains."

Mr. Antony laughed, and then said, "I give you my word for it, that is a real door."

"Have you ever opened it?"

“ Yes.”

“ Is any one inside ? ”

“ Not a living soul.”

“ Will there be any harm in it ? ”

“ None whatever.”

“ Then I’ll go.” She walked briskly to the door, though with secret trepidation. The moment she opened it, she started to find herself in a flood of saffron light; at the same instant, the door was suddenly closed behind her.

“ Oh, let me out,” cried she in a paroxysm of fear; but the next moment she was ashamed of herself, for she knew it could only be Mr. Antony who had shut her in. So she looked around her with admiration and awe. It was a small mausoleum to the memory of Lady Bourgeois, and only lighted by orange and purple glass. In a minute or two she tried the door again, and found it open; she re-entered the gallery, it was empty. At the farthest end of the most distant room, Mr. and Miss Antony, with their heads close together, were apparently absorbed in contemplation of a picture; but Nessy saw a little smile at the corner of Edith’s mouth.

"You shut me in!" said she to Mr. Antony. "What a shame!"

"Dear me," said he, with a pretended start, "have you come out of the tomb? I thought you never would come back!"

"*Is* it a tomb?"

"Something of the sort."

"I was not in it two minutes."

"My dear Miss Saffery, what are you thinking of? Half an hour, you mean. (He looked at his watch, and appeared to think himself confirmed in his statement.) You took no note of time. I suppose it passed as agreeably as it did to Father Felix in the 'Golden Legend,' who had a momentary peep, as he thought, into Paradise, which, in fact, lasted forty years."

"This was not Paradise."

"No; but the mausoleum of a very beautiful and beloved lady, full, I should think, of suggestive fancies."

"*Was* she beautiful and beloved?"

"No question of it."

"I don't believe," said Edith, "that you know any more about her than we do."

“ If she had been otherwise, would she have had such a mausoleum, think you ? ”

“ Perhaps not.”

And so their visit to the gallery ended. When they reached the place where the cart had been, the cart was there no longer. They all looked rather foolish. Presently, a turn of the road brought them to a gravel pit, and there was the cart with a horse in it : and there was a man shovelling gravel into the cart, and there were their things on the bank. The man laughed a little, and said—

“ I thought you’d find ’em.”

“ That was a very unwarrantable thought of yours,” said Mr. Antony ; “ and, to pay you off, I shall put you and your horse and cart and the gravel pit into my book.”

He very composedly set to work, till the man, who did not seem half to like it, filled his cart and drove it away ; and then they all walked on again.

“ I am sure there must be some story belonging to that deserted house,” said Mr. Antony. “ Some miser, perhaps, like old Elwes, lived in it. How I should have liked to tumble out all his hoards ! ”

"I thought you were not fond of money," said Nessy.

"Leonard not fond of money!" cried Edith. "Why, he's always thinking of it!"

"That I'm not!" said Leonard. "Only one can't entirely get on without it."

CHAPTER VIII.

THE DAILY ROUND.

WHAT a happy day it was! and though Nessy was very sorry to see the brother and sister go away, she had so much to think about that she was almost glad to be by herself, that she might live those happy, happy hours over again. She was not sorry to be sent to bed, where she could do so at her leisure; but she was so tired by her long walk, that she fell asleep directly she laid her head on her pillow, and did not even dream.

In the morning, Mrs. Saffery affixed a small white paper to the parlour window, bearing the single word "Lodgings." She and Nessy found plenty of work for themselves in taking up the carpet and giving the room a thorough cleaning. Mr. Antony had made Nessy a parting gift of sundry properties, not very valuable to himself, but of immense importance to her—

an old palette, a few brushes, some half-empty bottles of oil and varnish, sundry paints, and a piece or two of millboard. With these she intended to do wonders; and she very wisely resolved always to get her regular household tasks accomplished before she addressed herself to the fine arts. By this means she secured uninterrupted leisure, and escaped sundry scoldings that otherwise would certainly have fallen to her lot.

Nessy's life at this time was very happy; for Mr. Antony had so far given her a start, that she could pursue her course without immediately coming to a check. Of course her painting was what he or any other artist would have pronounced worthless; but neither she nor her parents were aware of this; so that she jogged on with a very comfortable belief that she was treading the very same path that 'Poussin and all the great ones had taken before her.

Her first check was the want of more paints, and though it was decided that she must and should have a fresh supply, they were not to be obtained till Mr. Saffery's next visit to London, which was not immediate. In the interim, Nessy had nothing to fall back upon but her sewing, over which she became very dreamy.

From this rather unhealthy state of mind she was roused unwillingly by the advent of a new lodger. Mrs. Puckeridge, the new comer, was by no means an agreeable lady. She was very self-indulgent, and her favourite indulgences were eating, drinking, lying in bed, and reading novels. It was a good thing for Nessy that she received a severe scolding for meddling with one of her books; for it was a wrong habit, which she required to be broken of, and the books were not good ones for her to read. The poor girl was starving, however, for want of mental aliment.

She grew so downhearted and absent, till now, Mrs. Saffery got into the way of scolding her, and saying, " Why, Nessy, you are not like the same girl ! Those painting-lessons spoilt you, I think."

" Oh, no," she would say, " they did me a great deal of good ; only I am losing all I learnt now, as fast as I can."

Then Mrs. Saffery told her husband that the paints must really be procured ; so Michael

Saffery brought his business affairs to a focus, and went up to London for the various things he wanted, not forgetting the paints.

When Nessy set to work again, it was as good as a play to hear Mrs. Puckeridge inveigh on the utter absurdity of a tradesman's allowing his daughter to paint in oils. Nessy would have fared badly, had she had to stand the brunt of her indignation by herself; but Mrs. Saffery came to the rescue with great effect, saying the lady must really pardon her, but she must beg leave to think herself the best judge of what was suitable for her own daughter. Nessy had property—a very pretty little property—and the tastes and inclinations of a lady; and, as long as they did not interfere with her domestic duties, which they had never done yet, it was her parents' desire that those tastes and inclinations should be cultivated.

Nessy had escaped into the kitchen, but she could not help hearing the above, and some more, through the open door; and when Mrs. Puckeridge said abruptly to her, the next time she went into the parlour, " What property have you ?" she coldly replied —

"Did not my mamma tell you, ma'am ?"

"No ; or I shouldn't have asked you."

"Then, since my mamma did not think proper to do so, I had better not," said Nessy.

"Oh, pray keep your own counsel, if you like. It's not of the least consequence," said Mrs. Puckeridge, in dudgeon. "I regret to have troubled myself to ask such an insignificant question. I suppose the ' property ' is so small that you are ashamed of mentioning it."

Nessy did not answer this taunt; and as she afterwards waited upon the indignant lady at dinner, in perfect and almost melancholy silence, she thought to herself that it might be possible she and her mother really did plume themselves too much on the thirty pounds a-year. It was the first time such a possibility had ever suggested itself to her.

The silence was broken in rather a ridiculous manner, for Nessy had to help Mrs. Puckeridge to some Scotch ale. The ale was "up," and sent the cork flying to the ceiling, and sprinkled Nessy's face, and made her involuntarily laugh a little, though she begged pardon the next instant. Mrs. Puckeridge drily remarked—

"People of property can't be expected to know how to draw a cork. I have property myself, and I never did anything so menial in my life, so of course *you* cannot be expected to. I rather prefer being waited on by servants who *are* servants, and not above their work, nor yet below it. I believe I shall quit these lodgings as soon as it suits my convenience; but not *before* it suits my convenience," she added quickly, as Nessy left the room.

"Mother," said Nessy, in a low voice, to Mrs. Saffery, "I cannot think how a lady can be as cross as Mrs. Puckeridge. She says she has property, but I don't think any amount of property can make up for such a temper."

"You are right, Nessy," said her mother; "money gives nobody a right to airs and ill-nature. Let it be a lesson to yourself. Your father and I are a little apt to spoil you sometimes—you are never snubbed—"

"Oh, yes, mamma!—by Mrs. Puckeridge."

"By *us*, I was going to say, if you had not interrupted. It's a bad habit of yours, Nessy, and proceeds from conceit. Mrs. Puckeridge, I was going to say, might, at your time of life,

have been as good a girl as yourself—there,
I did not mean that!"

"Thank you for it, though, mamma, all the
same."

"Well, you *are* a good girl, and that's the
long and short of it; only see, Nessy, what
even a good girl may come to, if she gets
spoilt, and has property, and never is snubbed."

"Only I don't know that Mrs. Puckeridge
ever *was* a good girl," said Nessy, "and can't
fancy it. There goes the bell. Is the pudding
ready?"

The pudding-sauce was not to Mrs. Puckeridge's mind, and her remarks on the person
who made it were unflattering. One way and
another, she contrived to make the Safferys'
gains by her very dearly earned; and Nessy
ardently hoped she would fulfil her threat of
going away. She did not do so for some
months, but when autumn came, and Hastings
became tempting, she gave notice to quit at
the week's end.

The family had never been so glad to be by
themselves. So quiet, and so cheerful! No
bell-ringing, no fault-finding, no meals but
their own to prepare. Mr. Saffery bought a

lobster for tea, because he said he thought they all deserved a treat after what they had put up with. As for Nessy, she now had leisure for the paints, which had long been in the house without her being able to use them ; for directly she began to lay her palette, Mrs. Puckeridge's little handbell was sure to ring. It had a peculiarly querulous tone, and she carried it from place to place with her wherever she lodged.

But now Nessy, with her mother's concurrence, placed her easel in the window of the unoccupied first-floor room, with a little three-legged table beside it on which she arranged her colours and brushes. Then, having completed her morning's work, and the dinner being cleared away, and her mother dressed and seated behind the counter with her plain work, and her father reading the *Times* in his arm-chair, still at the little dining-table in the parlour behind the shop,—and the shadows beginning to fall from west to east, and the whole village seeming steeped in quiet, so that you might hear the mewing of a stray kitten from one end of it to another—under these propitious circumstances did Nessy complacently take her stand before her easel, and, having long ago settled what she meant to do, begin to sketch with a piece of chalk on the sheet of primed millboard upon the trough the general features of the village-green ; the "Swan," with its yards, stables, coachhouses, and out-buildings—the old oak on its islet of verdure—the now leafless lane, winding out of sight—the baker's shop, the cottages, the gardens, pigsties, pigeon-houses, beehives—and the old man Mr. Antony had painted, sunning himself on a mossy bank.

It was a pretty, homely subject, prettily sketched. She started when her mother called her to get tea. Could it be four o'clock already? More than an hour fled before she could return to her darling task. Meantime, the shadows had surprisingly lengthened. The scene was prettier now than before.

With continual interruptions, yet with daily intervals of leisure, Nessy lovingly and perseveringly continued her task, till she had painted in a really attractive little oil-sketch. Of course, it was rude and full of faults and imperfections, and would have been utterly valueless in the estimation of a picture-dealer ; but still it pleased the eye—the unprofessional eye, at any rate.

Mr. and Mrs. Saffery viewed the performance with undisguised delight. It was put in the shop-window, and seen by every one in the village. Many were the encomiums which drew modest blushes into Nessy's cheeks, and made her heart overflow with pleasure. You may talk of your Raffaelles, Correggios, and stuff— she was as happy as any, or all of them. She could say, " I, too, am a painter."

The artist thrives on praise as the infant on milk and kisses ; but " solid pudding is better than empty praise," say you. Well ! suppose I tell you Nessy earned that too. A traveller, strolling round the green while the horses were changing, spied the picture, and, struck with the exact reproduction of details, went in and bought it of Mr. Saffery for seven-and-sixpence. Nessy was out at the time, and when she returned, was divided between disappointment at the loss of her picture and elation at its having been bought.

" Why, Mr. Antony sells his pictures, don't he ? " said Mr. Saffery. " Leastways, when he can. Don't be circumcilious, Nessy. Be thankful you can earn money, for it's not what all of 'em can do. As for your picture, you can paint another like it."

" I'm not quite sure I can," said Nessy, " but I'll try."

Her father held towards her the three half-crowns.

" Is it mine ?" said she, glowing with plea-sure. " May I have it all to myself ?"

" All to yourself? Yes, to be sure," said Michael Saffery. " You earned it yourself, and you may spend it yourself."

" Oh, thank you, father !—papa, I mean."

And our young lady of property took her three half-crowns more joyfully than poor Correggio his sackful of coppers.

CHAPTER IX.

THE UNCOMMON TASK.

JUST as Mr. Saffery and his daughter were thus standing with smiling faces at the counter, Mrs. Early, the poor widow-woman, whose son had gone to Australia, came in, looking more shabby and woebegone than ever, and anxiously said—

"Any letter for me, Mr. Saffery?"

"No, Mrs. Early," said he, still gaily.

She looked, almost with reproach, from one cheerful face to the other, and exclaimed, with passionate querulousness—

"Why don't he write?"

Then, bursting into tears, and covering her face with her hands, she hurried out of the shop.

"Oh, papa, it's very shocking!" said Nessy, piteously.

"Well, yes, so it is, poor creature!" said he;

"but what can we do? *We* can't make the thriftless scapegrace write."

" He must be a very bad son, I think," said Nessy.

" He may be dead," said Mr. Saffery.

One afternoon the letter-bag contained a dirty, foreign-looking letter, directed to " Mrs. Early, Providence Cottages, Belforest, Surrey, England," with a rather indifferent portraiture of Her Majesty on the stamp, which bore the superscription " Victoria, Sixpence."

" Why, here's a letter from George Early, I do suppose!" cried Mr. Saffery.

" Let me run down with it to her then, papa, please," said Nessy. " It will give Mrs. Early so much pleasure !"

" Off with you in a jiffy, then," said he, good-humouredly tossing it to her; and, putting on her garden-bonnet without even waiting to tie the strings, Nessy ran off to Providence Cottages. She tapped twice at the door before a stifled voice said, " Come in," and, when she entered, she saw Widow Early sitting on a low nursing-chair with her apron at her eyes.

" Mrs. Early, here's a letter for you," cried . Nessy, cheerfully. " A letter from Australia."

"Oh, you blessed, blessed girl!" exclaimed she, starting up, but instantly dropping again into her seat. "Give it me! give it me! He's alive, then?—thank God! I knew he'd write."

Her outstretched hand dropped feebly at her side. She faintly said, "My head is full of strange noises; everything dances before my eyes. Open the window, my dear, will you?"

Nessy did so, rather awe-stricken, and the fresh air revived the poor widow, who began to shed tears. She said, "Never mind, my dear, it relieves my head, and clears my sight —it is doing me good."

Then she imprinted two or three eager kisses on the letter, and began to open it with trembling hands, but she tore the thin paper with her nervous fingers, and Nessy said, "Let me cut round the seal for you," and produced her bright little scissors, which were tied to her side with a ribbon.

"Thank'e, my dear, thank'e kindly. I might have torn the writing. Why, how small he do write! and so little of it! and in such pale ink! Maybe there's a money-order in it. No, there isn't. Oh, dear me!—oh, dear!"

Her sigh was almost a sob ; and Nessy's quick thought was, "She is thinking more of money than of her son.   That is not right."

But, pitying the old woman, she said, " Have not you spectacles? shall I find them for you?"

" They're broken," said Mrs. Early, dolefully, " and I've no money to pay for their being mended. Oh, my dear, read me the letter, there's a good girl !   I don't suppose there are any secrets, and if there are, you must keep them faithfully."

" Oh, yes, I will," said Nessy.

So she took the letter, and read in a distinct, deliberate voice, while Mrs. Early, leaning towards her till their faces almost touched, devoured every word, as a famishing person devours food.

"My dear Mother,

"You will have fretted at my silence, and I would have written to you long ago, if I had had anything to tell which would give you pleasure. When I first came out, I had a bad fever, and while I was down with it, all my fellow-passengers went up the country, and the people I was with were thieves, and when I

got about again I had hardly a thing left. I
looked about for work, but could get none, and
there was nobody to speak for my character.
When half-starved, I consented to keep sheep
in the bush. It was quite a lonely life, away
from everybody and everything; and sometimes I seemed going out of my mind. After
this I gave up shepherding, and took some
bullocks across the country to another run.
This was more cheerful, as I had change of
scene and companions; but the scenery was, to
me, very melancholy, and my companions were
low, brutal fellows, and because I did not like
their talk, they made fun of me, and called me
the 'Young Lady.' I thought once or twice
I would make away with myself, but did not.
Then, at a public-house, we fell in with a lot
of fellows from the gold-diggings, and one of
them had found a nugget, he said, as big as
a beefsteak-pudding, and they told me I should
make a fortune in no time, so I determined to
go as soon as my engagement was ended. But
I had to do job-work first, to earn a little money
for the things I wanted; and once or twice I
was minded to write to you, only I knew you
would not like the diggings. So I thought I'd

put in for a nugget as big as a pudding, and when I'd got it I'd come home.

"However, I've been all this while at it, and have not found the nugget yet; and I have been ashamed to tell you of so many failures at one thing after another. One thing is certain—I don't like gold-digging at all. They are a horrid set of low fellows that do best at it, and I'm not even second-best. I've been ill, and been robbed, and been ill again. Some people were very kind to me last time, but they're gone away now.

"You must not think of coming out here; there is no chance of my building the pretty little cottage I promised you; I can't even send you a few pounds. My shirts and socks are dreadful, and prices are awful at the diggings. England is the best place for old people, and perhaps for young ones; but the human mind desires change. I kept my promise of saying that hymn every night, and reading my Bible on Sundays. Sometimes, though, in the bush, I did not know when Sunday came round. No churches nor church-bells. Oh! how gladly would I hear once more the ding-ding-dong of those three cracked

Belforest bells that I used to pretend said ' Come along, George!' I should think it the sweetest music."

Here he seemed to break off abruptly : the few lines in addition were dated some weeks later, from a place called Rummidumdumm, and merely contained these words—

" Off to the interior with an exploring-party, in search of rivers. We may come to grief : we may come to glory. Pray for me, mother dear ! May God bless you in this world and in the next.

" Your ever-affectionate son,

" GEORGE EARLY."

Mrs. Early, having held her breath to the end of the letter, now began to cry bitterly, and rock herself to and fro in the nursing-chair, saying—

" Oh, my son, my only boy ! He'll never come back, I know ! He'll perish in that howling wilderness ! "

" Oh, no, I hope not," said Nessy. " Perhaps they'll make some grand discovery."

But Mrs. Early shook her head and refused

to be comforted, saying, "His bones will whiten in the desert."

"It's a good thing he reads the Bible, at any rate," said Nessy, at which Mrs. Early stopped short. "What is the hymn he speaks of?"

"Ah, it's a good hymn that has strengthened many a sorrowful soul," said Mrs. Early. "I wouldn't let him rest till he got it by heart, and promised to say it on his pillow every night. It begins—let me see. Oh, this is it—

> "Commit thou all thy ways
> 　To His unerring hands,
> To His sure truth and tender care,
> 　Who earth and sea commands.
> No profit canst thou gain
> 　By self-consuming care,
> To Him commend thy cause, His ear
> 　Attends the softest prayer."

"I call that a very pretty hymn indeed," said Nessy. "I don't wonder at your son's repeating it. It's full of comfort, and I think if you would repeat it to me once or twice, I should know it too."

Mrs. Early repeated it once more, but would

not do so a third time; so, after Nessy had said, "Now, would not you rather have had this letter than that it should have gone to the bottom of the sea?" and extorted a reluctant, "Well, yes," she left her folding her hands and murmuring, "Praise the Lord that my boy wrote before he started! Pray God he may live to come back!" Her face looked peaceful as Nessy left her, yet it was so worn, withered, and shrivelled by age, watching, waiting, fasting, enduring all the unseen sorrows of penury and suspense, that the impression on Nessy was painful.

"Why, how long you have been!" said her mother, when she returned.

"I had to read the letter to Mrs. Early, as well as carry it to her," said Nessy. "Oh, mamma, she is so very, very poor! That clean little blind to the window makes people think there must be comfort within, but there was no fire. Instead of dinner, she was going to have tea; but only make-believe tea—toast-and-water poured out of a teapot. She had got the hot water of a neighbour."

"Dear me, that's very sad," said Mrs. Saffery. "I always fancied she was above want. Our used tea-leaves would be better for her than toast-and-water."

"Only she might be above having them," said Nessy. " But if you give me leave to offer them to her, I will."

" Her worthless son has a good deal to answer for," said Mrs. Saffery.

"Mamma, I don't know that he is worthless," said Nessy. "He says a hymn every night and reads his Bible on Sundays."

" Come, that's better than Mr. Antony, at any rate," said Mrs. Saffery.

Nessy did not like this remark, so she returned to George Early, and said—

"The only reason he did not write was, because he had no good news for his mother."

" He'd better have written, though, for all that," said Mrs. Saffery, "instead of wearing her heart out with suspense."

Mr. Saffery here came in from serving a customer, and said—

" Well, what has young Early been doing?"

" He has been gold-digging," said Nessy, " and now he has joined an exploring party, in search of inland rivers."

Mr. Saffery gave a sort of inward whistle, and said—

"Exploring parties are ticklish things."

After this, Nessy set about another picture, intending it for a facsimile of the first. For some reason or other it was not quite as good, and it was far from being a facsimile. The third attempt was better, and much smaller, because she had only small pieces of millboard left. These studies, and a succession of others, all of the same subject, were exhibited in due course, in the shop window, and, in due course, sold, at various prices; sometimes to a chance visitor at the inn, sometimes to a farmer or farmer's wife, and one or two were actually painted to order. Let no one think scorn of our young lady of property for exhibiting her works in the shop window, and receiving payment never reaching the dignity of gold. Except in idea, she was not in any way above her station, nor accustomed to think her parents demeaned themselves by selling tapes and stamping letters. She was naturally, or rather had become, fond of money, through having her "property" and "expectations" foolishly talked of; but she was beginning to have an idea that it was not the best thing in the world, nor even the most powerful. However, Nessy did not deal in abstract ideas, except after a fashion of her own. Mr. Antony had left behind him a crumpled envelop, much scribbled, which he had doubtless intended for the kitchen fire, but Nessy hoarded it as a treasure. It contained these scraps.

"Grey shades about the eyes give an air of modesty.

"Sir Joshua told his pupils, when painting flesh tints, to think of a pearl and a peach.

"Lord Palmerston said the other day, that some men think the human mind is like a bottle, and that when you have filled it with anything, you can pour it out and leave it as empty as before. That, however, quoth his lordship, is not the nature of the human mind. No, indeed, I wish it were, in some things.

"The Bishop of Troyes, in his funeral eulogium on Prince Jerome Buonaparte, called him 'assez religieux.' Ha, ha! Good, that.

"'Il y a des paroles qui valent les meilleures actions, parceque, en germe, elles les contiennent toutes.' Regulus's 'no,' for example?"

Nessy, though she did not understand half

of any one of these aphorisms, nor know what was original, what only quoted, had a glimmering notion that they were clever, and that it was a good plan to secure one's fugitive thoughts, if they had any good or beauty, before they were lost. But when she tried to write down some of her own, she could not, for a time, find any.

I do not wish to tell tales of Michael Saffery, but certainly he was fond of news fresh from the press, and certainly he made no scruple of daily reading the *Times* as it passed through his hands to some subscriber. One day, when thus engaged, he called to Nessy—

"Here's something that will interest Mrs. Early, maybe. Come and read it, and then you can tell her about it."

It was a short paragraph extracted from an Australian paper, mentioning the exploring expedition, and the interest and sympathy it had excited, and the dangers it would probably have to face. The names of the explorers were given, including that of George Early, though as a subordinate.

It was better for Mrs. Early to hear Nessy's version of the paragraph, than to read the original, for Nessy would be too kind and discreet to dwell on the probable dangers. She undertook the mission with pleasure, and, on tapping at the door, heard "come in" uttered with more alacrity than the first time; for Mrs. Early now knew her tap. "Another letter?" cried she eagerly, as Nessy entered.

"No," said Nessy, "but—" The widow dejectedly sat down in the nursing-chair.

"But," pursued Nessy, "there is mention of your son in the *Times* newspaper."

"Has he found the river? has he got glory?" cried Mrs. Early.

"Not yet, but very likely he will. You can't think how interested the gentry and townspeople were in the expedition. They gave the explorers all manner of useful and portable things to take with them—more, at last, than they could carry; preserved meats, and fruits, and all sorts—and started them off, and gave them three cheers at parting. Was not that nice?"

"What does it amount to," said Widow Early, "if they leave their bones to bleach in the desert?"

Having got this idea into her head, there

was no getting it out, except by reverting to a subject nearer home.

"And here's Mr. Broad, Miss Saffery," said she disconsolately (Mr. Broad was her landlord), "says he won't let me be here after Saturday, for he's going to raise the rent. I must go into the House."

"Oh, I hope not," cried Nessy.

"But I *must*," she reiterated, crying bitterly, "for I can't hold up my head any longer, and there's no other place to go to. Living on dry bread and toast-and-water lowers one's strength, so that one can't struggle on and on for ever. I must go into the house, though I never thought I should, for I've known better days."

Now, it so happened, that Mrs. Prosser had lately given up the White Cottage, which, with some of its least valuable furniture, had been put up to auction; and, as nobody 'else happened to want it, it had been knocked down a dead bargain to Mr. Saffery, who thought it would be a very good investment for Nessy, and sure to let in the summer. They had been looking about for some one to put in it and keep it open.

Nessy was delighted at being, in any sense,

the proprietress of the White Cottage (the rent of which was fifteen pounds), and she now hastened home to beg her parents to let Mrs. Early be the person put in to take care of it. They had previously decided on the allowance that was to be given, which, though slender, would be something to Mrs. Early.

Mr. and Mrs. Saffery did not at first take kindly to the proposal, but Nessy dwelt with glowing cheeks and dilated eyes on the sore strait of the poor widow, and the great advantage it would be to her, till they saw it with her eyes, and at length consented.

Joyfully did Nessy return to Mrs. Early to tell her of her preferment, and very sweet was it to her to see how glad and thankful it made her. The removal from Providence Cottages was now looked forward to, not with dismay, but with pleasure; true, her position there might not be permanent, but while it lasted it was a pure, unqualified good; and, for once in her life, Mrs. Early would not look forward to evil.

"If George could see me here," said she, complacently, at her neat little tea-table, when Nessy looked in on her on Saturday afternoon, "he'd think me in no need of a squatter's hut. I fancy there are not many cottages in Australia as pretty as this."

She spoke quite at random; for she knew nothing of Australia but the name.

CHAPTER X.

DISAPPOINTMENT.

NESSY at length produced a *chef d'œuvre*, in the opinion of the family; and Mrs. Saffery exclaimed, "Mr. Antony ought to see this!"

"Oh, mamma!" said Nessy, in affright.

"Yes, I don't see why he shouldn't," said Mr. Saffery. "Yet, on the other hand, why should he? He sees plenty of good pictures every day."

"That don't signify," rejoined Mrs. Saffery. "He started Nessy off at it, and he'll be glad to see the progress she has made."

"Yes, I should think he would be," said Mr. Saffery, doubtfully. "But how shall you get it to him?"

"In a deal packing-case, to be sure," said his practical wife, "such as he used to pack his own pictures in. I've an old one upstairs, that will only want some wedges to make the painting fit it. Go you, and fetch it down, Nessy."

Now that the first shock at the scheme was over, Nessy's heart beat high with elation. She felt quite sure, at that moment, that hers was a wonderful performance, and that Mr. Antony would be very much surprised and delighted.

"You must write a line with it, Nessy," said her mother, as she proceeded to fit the wedges.

"Oh, mother !—what shall I say ?"

"Only that we thought he would like to see how well you paint now."

Nessy could not say so thus broadly, though it was the very thing she meant to express. With a great deal of preparation and forethought, and copying from the slate, she completed the following note :—

"SIR,

"My mamma thinks you may like to see what progress I have made since you left. I am afraid it is done rather badly.

"With our best respects to Miss Antony,
I am, Sir,
"Your obedient servant,
"NESSY SAFFERY."

She was not quite sure this was as a lady would have expressed it, and she wistfully read it again and again, to see whether she could improve it, but found she could not; and really she had said all that was wanting, and no more. Her father carried the case, duly directed, to the station; and Nessy followed him with her eyes till he turned the corner, full of silent exultation. This lasted till he came back—till the train was off; all that time she seemed walking on air.

Then the bubble broke; the balloon collapsed; she was no longer buoyed up by her imaginings; she felt perfectly vapid and flat. She was quite certain Mr. Antony would think the picture the greatest daub that ever was painted, and the note presumptuous and absurd. Nessy was ready to cry all the rest of the evening, and she lay awake half the night.

Mr. and Mrs. Saffery little knew what the poor girl endured during the next two days. Of course she was a gratuitous self-tormentor; but the torment was none the less real.

When the post came in on the evening of the second day, Mr. Saffery, who was sorting the letters by candlelight, called out to Nessy in a lively tone, " A letter for you, Nessy ! "

She darted from the parlour into the shop. "Oh, where, papa ? " and joyously seized it. She tore it open with nervous fingers. It only contained two words—

" Capital! capital ! "

Nessy's heart gave a great bound. Her first feelings were of relief and thankfulness. He had seen, had approved, had encouraged. Then came a great recoil. How short ! how unsatisfying ! how disappointing a letter ! Perhaps he was only laughing at her ! This thought was intolerable ; she chased it from her, and yet it would recur.

When Mrs. Saffery came in, it was with very subdued complacence that Nessy said, " Mr. Antony has written, mamma."

" Well, what has he said ? " rejoined Mrs. Saffery.

" He says, ' Capital, capital.' "

" Well, that *is* capital," said her mother. "But only those two words ? He need not have been so sparing, I think."

" Only those two words," said Nessy, sighing.

Next morning the picture reached her. Just

as she was taking it from its case, a lady came in to buy something: the rector's wife, Mrs. Fownes.

"Dear me, that's a pretty little thing," said she. "Did you do it, Miss Saffery?"

Nessy owned the soft impeachment.

"Why, you must be a self-taught genius. I should think you might get a medal from the Society of Arts. Would not you like to do so?"

"Yes, I dare say I should, ma'am," said Nessy, contemplating public honours for the first time.

"Well, you've nothing to do but to write to the secretary, and send up your picture. I don't exactly know the steps, but you could easily learn them of any friend in London. It's about the time, I think, for sending the pictures in."

Mr. Saffery was caught by this: a good deal of talk ensued; and Nessy felt the dawning of a new ambition. Whether it were for her good or not, I don't pretend to say. I rather think the simple girl only dreamed of shining in the eyes of her father, her mother, and Mr. Antony. It was decided, in family conclave, that she must write to him again. Nessy had a great repugnance to doing so. She was not sure how he had taken her first note, nor whether irony lurked in his " capital, capital." She remembered the severe things he had said of her writing, and she feared it was not much better now. It was, however.

After almost as much thought as if it were an Act of Parliament, she wrote as follows :—

" Belforest, March 7.

" SIR,

" I am afraid this second note may be intrusive ; but our rector's lady, Mrs. Fownes, has recommended me to send my picture to the Society of Arts, Manufactures, and Commerce, Adelphi, Strand ; and my papa and mamma wish me to be guided by your advice. Perhaps you do not think it good enough. There are gold and silver prizes, of various sizes, given. Of course I could only hope for the smallest silver one. Apologizing for this liberty, I am, sir, with our united respects,

" Your obedient servant,

" NESSY SAFFERY."

In two days Nessy received the following answer :—

K 2

" Newman Street, March 10.

" Dear Miss Saffery,

" Considering the circumstances of the case,
I think your picture quite as worthy of the
Isis medal as many that have obtained it ; at
any rate, you can but try. 'Aim highly, fall
nobly,' is the best motto. Your painting is a
very creditable little performance. As you are
a long way from town, and my time is rather
fully occupied, my sister will, if you wish it,
take the necessary steps, on your sending up
the picture. Honorary rewards, though not
very valuable in themselves, are spurs to us,
along what Sir E. Bulwer Lytton calls 'the
upward course of an opposed career ;' and
there is no reason why you should not put
in for them if you like it. Kind regards to
Mr. and Mrs. Saffery.

"Yours, &c.

"Leonard Antony."

This letter made Nessy very happy. She
did not mind its qualified and rather super-
cilious tone ; that was characteristic of Mr.
Antony. He had once, and only once, been
surprised into saying she had genius ; but it
had sent a thrill through her as the same thing

said by Sir Egerton Brydges' father sent a thrill through the sensitive son. Then, again, Mr. Antony had put her in connexion with his sister, with whom Nessy felt much more at ease, though she had only been in her company a few hours : she was altogether a more eligible correspondent for her. This affair caused a good deal of pleasant family conversation ; all were hopeful, though none of them immoderately so.

After Nessy had sent her picture a second time on its travels, she received a very kind note from Edith, inclosing a list of printed rules, and telling her that she should have affixed a card to her painting, with the sex, age, name, and class of the artist written on it. "I mean," she continued, "whether you belong to the honorary or artist class. Of course, the former, as you are not professional, and have never sold your paintings."

Here was a sudden check. Nessy *had* sold paintings : she *was* professional. "Oh, what a pity ! " she exclaimed, half aloud. But then she thought, "what difference does it make ? I don't mind their thinking me not quite a lady, and that is all the difference."

No, it was not; but Nessy did not know it. She wrote Edith a plain statement of the fact, that she had sold many little pictures as soon as they were painted.

"*Here's* even-handed justice for you!" said Mr. Antony, grimly, when his sister told him of it. "Nessy Saffery can sell her pictures, and I can't sell mine."

Nessy now tasted a little of the cup of suspense—not its dregs, but its edge. Other people's conjectures and anticipations had made of moment to her what would otherwise never have occurred to her to wish for. She would not like to fail, now that Mr. and Miss Antony and Mrs. Fownes knew all about it, and her father and mother spoke of it across the counter to this and that country neighbour. "Our Nessy has sent a picture to the exhibition, at least to an exhibition. Our Nessy has a picture in a picture-gallery. Our Nessy is trying for a prize."

All this made harder the disappointment in store for her, when her feverish little day-dream was dispelled. Edith wrote a kinder note than ever, saying she was very sorry to tell Miss Saffery that her picture was (Edith would not write the grating word rejected, but) not accepted. She could quite feel for her disappointment, for she had had disappointments herself; but she had always found the best way to get over them was not to rate the thing missed above its real worth, and to turn the attention to something else as soon as possible. "Happily you are not, as many artists are, dependent on your talents for support," she wrote; "and, even supposing you to be so, why, your being able to sell your pictures as you do, shows you can suit the popular taste; and the real test of a book or a picture is its being *bought*, whatever the critics may say of it. When people are willing to pay for a thing, you may be pretty sure they really want to have it, and value it. So you have more reason to be glad your pictures sell, than you would have had if one particular picture had procured you a medal. At least, that is one view of the subject. A member of the society told me you would have had a fair chance if you had been able to class yourself as an honorary candidate, because an artist is supposed to have had professional training (which you have not), and is therefore more severely judged."

"How kind she is!" Nessy thought; but

her lip quivered and she twinkled away a tear. She was in the little back parlour by herself when she opened the letter, and she felt very much inclined to run up to her attic and have a snug cry before she faced her father and mother. However, like little Abner Brown, she "took a 'poonful of resolution," and bravely went to her mother, and said,

"Mamma, I've had a disappointment. My picture is not considered good enough for a prize."

"Dear heart, what a pity!" said Mrs. Saffery, who was clear-starching. "What could be the matter with it, I wonder?"

"I don't know that anything was the matter with it," said Nessy; "but it was put along with others that were a great deal better, being done by real artists."

"Then yours should not have been put along with theirs, that's clear," said Mrs. Saffery. "It was not fair."

"Ah, but every society has its rules," said Nessy, checking a sigh; "and I dare say it was all fair enough. Miss Antony seems to think so : she writes very kindly."

"Let me hear what she says," said her mother.

Nessy read the letter, and Mrs. Saffery re-marked,

"That's a very good letter, and one that you may take pride in her having written to you. I must say, Nessy, you take the disappointment very well; and I am pleased with you."

This quite paid the simple girl, who went cheerfully to tell her father. She said less, and he said less than had passed between her and Mrs. Saffery; his sole remark being,

"Oh, it's rejected, is it? Well, what can't be cured, must be endured. There is generally a good deal of favouritism in those matters. I told you, I thought you would not get it" (which was quite a mistake of his), "and you'll soon forget all about it. As soon as the picture is put in the shop window, it will be sure to sell."

Mrs. Saffery had been the best consoler, and Nessy asked her leave to answer Miss Antony's kind letter, which she felt would be a soothing employment. Leave obtained, she wrote to this effect—

"DEAR MISS ANTONY,   "Belforest.

"I think it very kind. of you to send me such a nice letter. I have quite got over my disappointment now, though it was one, of course, and shall turn my attention to other things, only remembering your kindness. Pray forgive my having caused you so much trouble. My papa and mamma desire their best respects to be sent to you and Mr. Antony, and I remain

"Yours respectfully and truly obliged,

"NESSY SAFFERY."

"Poor little wretch! it must have been a disappointment to her," remarked Mr. Antony; "but she takes it very sensibly. Do you think she would like to see the prizes given away? I could get her a ticket."

"How can you think of anything so tantalizing?" said Edith. "Much better let her forget all about it. She does not need honorary rewards, and I am not at all sure that emulation is, in any case, a good thing."

"Oh, indeed!" (Ironically.)

Whether the attempt to compete with others had done Nessy harm or no, I am persuaded her failure, in so far as it humbled her, did her real good; for it did not amount to a crushing mortification, but only made her take a more moderate and just estimate of herself. She found she was a nobody among artists, though, among those who were not, she was held to paint pictures rather prettily.

About this time it happened that Mrs. Saffery discovered Nessy's old bed-furniture would hold together no longer, and she told her she would give her new dimity if she would make the furniture herself. Nessy was delighted, and obtained the additional grant of a daisy-fringe, and, after that, a remnant of pink glazed calico to cover a light table, with a clear muslin toilette-cover over it, so that she made her attic quite smart. All this pleasant employment set painting quite aside, and a variety of other wholesome domestic engagements enabled Nessy's head to clear itself of too dominant a subject, and her mind to recover its healthy tone. Sometimes she looked in on Mrs. Early, who did not now come incessantly to inquire for letters, as she knew that her son could not write to her during his exploring journey; but she was very greedy of a little chat about him with Nessy, who, to gratify her, had borrowed one or two books on Australia, and picked up a few facts about it to retail to her; but she never succeeded in convincing Mrs. Early that it was not a howling wilderness peopled with howling savages, with grass as brown as hay, and salt-marshes instead of rivers.

All connexion with the Antonys now seemed at an end, and Nessy was therefore surprised as well as pleased when, about the beginning of June, she received a note from Edith, saying that, as the weather was now so pleasant, she and her brother were thinking of spending a day in the country, and would be glad, if convenient, to bring a friend with them to see the Dulwich Gallery, and afterwards dine at Mr. Saffery's.

As the lodgings were unlet, they were quite at the Antonys' service, and Mrs. Saffery was glad to requite Edith's kindness to Nessy by her alacrity in engaging to have everything comfortable, in a plain way, for the party. It was delightful to Nessy to put up the clean blinds, gather flowers for the chimneypiece, and assist in the preparations.

"I wonder whether the friend is a lady or gentleman," said Mrs. Saffery. "Ducks and green peas and gooseberry-pie will do for either; but one would like to know. Perhaps

it is some gentleman that is going to marry
Miss Antony; or it may be some young lady
who is going to marry Mr. Antony."

"It ought to be a very nice gentleman for
Miss Antony," said Nessy, "or a very nice lady
for Mr. Antony. I wonder what sort of lady
he would like."

"A lady with a good bit of money, most
likely," said her practical mother.

"I did not mean that," said Nessy. "I meant
whether tall or short, dark or fair, and so on."

"Ah! looks are but skin deep," said Mrs.
Saffery. "If you had ten thousand pounds,
Nessy, people wouldn't mind how plain you
were."

This remark made Nessy thoughtful. She
habitually plumed herself on her thirty pounds
per annum; but yet, to be run after merely
because she had ten thousand pounds, would
be running after what she held, not what she
was, any more than you run after the dog who
has run away with your dinner; you run after
your leg of mutton.

CHAPTER XI.

ROSABEL.

THE first glimpse of the expected visitors showed that the stranger was a lady—a young lady—a pretty young lady—a tall, pretty young lady, prettily dressed. Nessy saw all this at one eager glance, and next she saw that Mr. Antony, much better dressed than usual, though she could not say in what respect, looked almost—nay, more than handsome. His cheek, his eye, his mouth, his whole air, the tone of his voice, told that he was under some spell or excitement. Edith, who hung a little back, and was prettily, though inexpensively dressed, looked languid and tired. Nessy's face lighted up when their eyes met, and Edith's face cleared directly she saw the grateful girl : each instantly felt there was sympathy between them.

"Ah, Nessy—Miss Saffery!" said Mr. Antony, hastily correcting himself, "how do you do?

Here we are, you see, a little after the time appointed. The ladies would like to leave some of their wraps here before we go to the Gallery—they fancied it might rain."

Nessy's answer was a bright, silent smile. She had shaken hands with Edith, who was friendly, and treated her more like an equal than her brother did. Nessy had thought he would name the young lady to her, but he did not. She had settled in an instant, that here was Mr. Antony's future wife; but she had not settled that she liked her.

She showed them into the neat little parlour.

"Here are my old quarters, you see, Miss Bell," said Mr. Antony, with an attempt at unconcern that was not quite successful. "Capital ones, too, for a bachelor. Don't you think small rooms are snug?"

Miss Bell didn't know : she preferred large ones. She said this in a thin, rather high voice, that had no melody in it. Edith untied her bonnet and took it off, and began to smooth her hair, which the wind had a little ruffled.

"Would you like to step upstairs, Miss Antony, and have a comb?" said Nessy, lingering.

"Yes, I think I should," said Edith. "Will you come, Miss Bell?"

"No; I do very well, thank you," said Miss Bell. "Nobody to see one, you know."

"Oh, then, I won't go," said Edith, resuming her bonnet.

"Pray do, Edith, if you want to," said her brother.

"Oh, no; it does not signify."

Meanwhile Nessy had disappeared; and presently Mrs. Saffery entered, bearing a tray with cake and some home-made wine, while Nessy brought a china jug of water.

"Oh, we didn't mean to lunch, thank you," said Edith. "Will you take anything, Miss Bell?"

"I should like a biscuit."

"You will spoil those pretty gloves, if you don't take them off," observed Mr. Antony. However, she did not offer to remove them. "Won't you have something, Edith?"

"Only a glass of water. How deliciously cold it is! and so sparkling! so different from London water."

"Some wine, Miss Bell?"

"No, thank you."

"Just a little—"

"No, thank you ; I never drink home-made wines.   We never have them."

Mr. Antony looked a little annoyed.   "We are going to the Dulwich gallery, Miss Saffery," said he to Nessy, as she was leaving the room. "Would you like to go with us ? "

Edith gave him a quick look, and so did Miss Bell.   Nessy blushed with pleasure and embarrassment, and said, "I fear I should intrude, sir."

"No, no, not at all," said he.   "We shall be glad to have you.   *Shall* we not ? " appealing to his companions.

"Of course," said Edith.   Miss Bell looked as if she had no concern in the question.

"Do go, then," said he, cheerfully.   "At least, if you like it."

"Oh, yes, sir ! I should like it very much."

And away she hastened to obtain her mother's consent, and put on her Sunday things.   Edith said, with a smile, when she was gone, "You left me no choice but to say ' of course,' in her hearing."

"Why, there was nothing else to say, was there ?   Do *you* mind her going, Miss Bell ? "

"It makes no difference to me, either way."

"No, I supposed it would not ; and we shall give the poor child a little pleasure. Her life is dull enough."

"She does not look as much a child as she did," said Edith. "She is grown, and grown prettier."

"No—has she? I did not notice. She may have grown, but can hardly have grown pretty. Miss Bell, that plain little girl is a genius. Do you admire geniuses ? "

"Oh, yes ! very much," said Miss Bell ; "they are so entertaining."

"Not always, I'm afraid. Some are very grave and profound."

"They are very disagreeable."

"Oh, no ! " said Edith ; and she took up the defence of profound geniuses with animation, to which Miss Bell answered in monosyllables of assent or dissent ; while Mr. Antony, lapsing into silence, attentively observed her profile. It was Grecian, but the expression was very insipid; and nothing less than the misleading imagination of a young artist-lover could have tricked this inane young lady with the attributes of a semi-goddess, though her teeth were like pearls, and her eyes limpid blue. Nessy, fresh as a flower, entered before he was tired of his long, unreproved gaze, which Miss Bell was quite conscious of, though she appeared not to be.

"Oh, now we had better be off, then," said he, starting up, and giving a quick look at Nessy. The result was an inward concession of "Yes, she's prettyish. Mind begins to give expression."

As soon as they were all in the open air, a spell seemed suddenly removed. At first, they all walked in a line, four abreast, in the middle of the country-road, in the following order :— Nessy, Edith, Miss Bell, Mr. Antony. Edith, whose glimpses of the country were not many, but who was extremely fond of it, immediately began to say droll and cheerful things, which her brother answered with spirit, glancing at Miss Bell every time for a smile, or laugh, or assenting look. Nor were they denied, for though she said little, she looked pleased, and seemed to enjoy the harmless puns and witticisms that are pretty sure to occur when a party of lively young people take a country walk together. If one or two of them happen to have what passes current for wit among those who are not too captious, there is no need for all to be droll, so that they are but *en rapport* with each other. Nessy had never heard such a flow of repartee before; she thought it delightful; and though Miss Bell only smiled when she might have laughed, and often let a point escape her altogether, she seemed waking up so fast from her torpid fit, that Nessy, catching a glimpse of her across Edith now and then, began to think her pretty.

Presently, they turned off the high-road, and were treading the elastic turf of the undulating upland which commanded the scene of Nessy's sketch.

"Nessy!—Miss Saffery!—why, here is 'The Escape of Pyrrhus!'" cried Mr. Antony, laughing; and he began to tell Miss Bell, in a lively, pleasant way, about Nessy's historical flight, and her heroic sacrifice.

Miss Bell smiled, and looked at Nessy rather curiously, remarking, "It was a pity to burn it."

Nessy walked onwards in a happy reverie, overpaid for the immolation by Mr. Antony's glowing words. He had said, "She did not know how well she had done it."

"A great shame of you not to have told her, then," said Edith. "What a pretty cottage that is in the dell!"

"That's mine," said Nessy.

"*Yours?*" said they all.

"Yes; my papa thought it a good investment."

They gave a quick look at one another, and Miss Bell was ready to laugh.

"Is she rich, then?" said she aside to Mr. Antony.

"She has property," returned he in the same tone, delighted to have this shadow of a confidence.

If Nessy could have read Miss Bell's thoughts, she would have known that in her estimation she had risen from a nobody to a somebody.

They went on, up and down the little inequalities of the ground, for a short time in silence, and then Edith inquired—

"Are you going to live there?"

"Oh, no! we hope to let it."

"Don't you hope to live in it some of these days?"

"Oh, no! we could not afford it.   The post-office does well enough for us."

Nessy sank from her temporary elevation in Miss Bell's opinion.

"Is it empty now?" inquired Edith.

"Mrs. Early is in it, to keep it open."

"Mrs. Early! I seem to remember that name," said Mr. Antony.

"Yes, sir, the person who used to come so frequently to ask for a letter from her son, and who always said, 'Why don't he write?'"

"Oh, ay—and does she go on saying so still?"

"No, sir; he *has* written."

"Indeed!"

"She was so glad," said Nessy, with feeling. "I took her the letter, and she trembled so, she could not open it, nor yet read it; so I read it to her, and it explained how he came not to have written to her sooner; and he said he was going into the interior with an exploring party, in search of rivers."

"Dear me! that is very interesting," said Edith.   "He may make some great discovery."

"Or perish in the wilderness," said Mr. Antony.

" That's what Mrs. Early said," observed Nessy. " She said his bones would bleach in the desert."

" I like that cottage, with its tall white lilies, very much," said Edith ; " I should like to live in it."

" I wish you did, Miss Antony," said Nessy.

" Should *you* like to live in a cottage ? " said Mr. Antony in a low voice to Miss Bell. " Could you be happy in one ? "

" Oh dear, yes, if it were covered all over with honeysuckle and passion-flower ! I should delight in it."

He looked earnestly at her, and began to hum *sotto voce*, at first without the words—

> " O Nanny, wilt thou gang with me,
>   Nor sigh to leave the flaunting town ?
>   Can silent vales have charms for thee,
>   The lowly cot, the russet gown ? "

" That's a sweet thing," said Miss Bell. " The sentiment is so pretty. It goes so well to the harp."

" The harp is a divine instrument."

" I don't like it nearly as much as the piano, though," said Edith.

Her brother uttered an impatient groan of dissent.

"No, no more do I," said Miss Bell. "And I should not like a russet gown. Brown is so very ugly."

"The russet gown of the ballad only typifies simple tastes," said Mr. Antony. "Even poor people don't wear russet now."

"Russet-coloured alpacas are worn sometimes," said Edith; but this prosaic observation elicited no remark. Mr. Antony was expatiating on simple tastes to Miss Bell; and, as their route now lay through a rutty lane, with a very narrow footpath, they fell into couples; Mr. Antony and Miss Bell in advance, and Edith and Nessy behind them, stopping from time to time to gather wild flowers. Edith was very desirous to know the name of every herb and flower that grew in hedge and field, and was soon learning of Nessy the names of wood-sorrel, stitch-wort, golden-rod, shepherd's-purse, and shepherd's-needle. They came to a pause over their nosegays, but Edith, looking up and seeing the others a good way in advance, ran after them, and Nessy after her, without stopping for some of the dropped flowers. Mr. Antony and his companion seemed to have made progress in the interim; they were talking together with ease and apparent interest, and the narrowness of the lane still kept Edith and Nessy behind, till they took their position as a matter of course, and did not think of altering it as the path widened. To Nessy this was delightful : she had never had such a congenial, yet superior companion, before; one to whom she could admiringly look up, yet who did not put her down. Edith's disposition was excellent; she was frank, kind, and unselfish, with a keen appreciation of what was good and beautiful in nature and art. Even about wild flowers she seemed to put Nessy's vague thoughts into words—better words than would ever have occurred to her. When they came to an end of the subject, Nessy said, after a little pause—

"Are you not very fond of reading, Miss Antony? *I* am; so very fond!"

"I am not fond of reading for reading's sake," said Edith; "there are other things which I often like better; but when I get a book that suits me, I certainly enjoy it thoroughly."

"Would you tell me some of the books you like?" said Nessy timidly.

"There are so many," said Edith, laughing. "I am very fond of travels, and lives of painters, and essays and poems, and magazines, and good, healthy, spirited novels."

"None of those books come in my way," said Nessy, "so I am obliged to content myself with what I can get."

"What have you?"

"'Sacred Dramas,' and 'The Death of Abel.' Those were prize-books. And Butler's 'Astronomy,' and the 'Grecian History,' and the 'History of England.' Those were lesson-books. And Bingley's 'Animal Biography,' and 'Prince Lee Boo,' and the 'Gentleman's Magazine.' Those are my father's."

"Poor child—and can you really be fond of such books as those?"

"There are some nice things in them," said Nessy, "but I own I'm too fond of picking out the plums."

"*Are* there any plums in the old Gentleman's Magazine? I thought it was only what school-boys call stodge."

"Oh, no!" said Nessy, laughing, "there are

some very good pickings here and there ; especially in the obituary."

"Well, you have the oddest taste! Let us run ; they are getting on so fast."

Arrived at the gallery, they once more united in a group, but soon scattered, as people do when they are looking at pictures. Mr. Antony, however, was continually going off to something else, and then saying, " Come and look at this, Miss Bell," and then she would affect to be more reluctant, Nessy thought, than she really was, but yet went ; and when Edith and Nessy joined them, they found they were not talking of the pictures at all, nor even looking at them, which Edith was the less surprised at, because they were often the poorest in the gallery. She grew tired of this, at last, and a little cross, and gave up following them about ; straying from one to another of her favourite pictures, and looking at them absently. Nessy, who at first enjoyed following the bent of her own taste, was insensibly drawn to her admired companion, whom she preferred even to the pictures. Seeing Edith looking fixedly at David with Goliath's head, she said—

" Is this a good picture, Miss Antony ? "

"Yes—no;" said Edith. "You know it is by your favourite Poussin."

"Perhaps these pictures don't improve on acquaintance?"

"They ought to do so. What makes you suppose so?"

"I don't think Mr. Antony seems to find they do."

A look that crossed Edith's face made Nessy feel she had better have spared the remark, though she could not think what harm there was in it. To make the matter better or worse, she added—

"Nor do you."

"Oh, I like them very well," said Edith, "only I'm tired, and thinking of other things. Ah! they are looking at Rubens' Mother. Let us admire it too."

Mr. Antony, however, was not looking at Rubens' Mother, but at Miss Bell, and as they approached him from behind, Nessy heard him softly call her "Rosabel."

Miss Bell, who saw them coming, let a look of extreme coldness take place of a downcast softness, as she said rather drily—

"My name is not Rosabel, but Rosa, and I

don't like being called by my Christian name."
Saying which, she placed herself beside Edith,
and continued to attach herself to her all the
rest of their stay in the gallery, which was not
very long. Mr. Antony looked taken a little
aback, and the rest of the dialogue was disjointed and pointless.

CHAPTER XII.

THE COTTAGE.

It was now full time they should make the best of their way homewards, unless they meant the ducks and green peas to be spoilt; but Mr. Antony, with the wilfulness of his tribe, saw fit to discover an excellent point for a sketch, and nothing would prevent him from taking it.

There are, or were, many pretty little rural bits about Dulwich and Norwood, such as Ruysdael would have loved. The present one would hardly figure much in description. The turn of a rutty road, a broken, gravelly bank, tufted with weeds, a broken paling, a little ragged copse, with deep shadows between the slender trunks, a gleam of water, that was in fact only a pool, a cow standing under a tree, and lowing for her calf, another cow audibly cropping the grass, fleecy clouds overhead—there was not much more.

Mr. Antony, however, plopped down on the grass, and out with his book, in spite of Edith's " Dinner will certainly be spoilt."

"Do you take one of the cows, then, and Miss Saffery the other," said he ; " they may move away, which the landscape will not. At present, the pose is excellent."

"I've no pencil," observed Nessy.

"Help yourself," said he, holding out a handful to her, and then to Edith. Edith wanted paper and a penknife ; he supplied both ; there was no getting off, so there were they, three in a row, all sketching very earnestly, while Miss Bell twined her hat with eglantine.

"Miss Bell, you come in very well," said Mr. Antony. " I will put you in."

Miss Bell was quite agreeable, and put herself a little in attitude, which he accused her of, and she denied ; so that made a little laughing. One way and another, they were all very happy.

"Which cow will you have, Miss Antony ? " said Nessy.

"The lowing one, please," said Edith. ". I hope she won't leave off yet."

"Am I to put in the brown spots ? " said Nessy.

"Every one of them," said Mr. Antony, "and plenty of tail."

"Oh, I do believe my cow is going to lie down!"

At the same moment, the other, ceasing to low, wildly dashed along the hedge to another gate, making all the ladies start to their feet in fear of a collision. Mr. Antony did no good after this; finding which, he put up his tools, and away they went merrily. It was one of those little episodes that one takes no note of, and yet it marked with a white stone that day in his life.

Arrived at the post-office, they found dinner done to a turn, and Mrs. Saffery rather anxiously awaiting them. Miss Bell thought it odd that a young person of property should change their plates, &c., but to every one else it appeared quite simple. After dinner it became a question what to do next. They were too tired to go far, and Mr. Antony voted for going on with his sketch while they talked to him, which they pronounced very stupid.

"Miss Saffery, might not we go over your cottage?" said Edith.

"Oh, yes; do, please!"

"Nobody is in it, I think you said?"

"No one but Mrs. Early."

So off they went, and Mrs. Early, in her neat, close cap and faded black gown, received them with smiles; but her cheeks were very thin, poor woman! for the fact was she had too little to eat. The trifle she received for keeping the cottage open was nearly all she had to live upon; but she was allowed plenty of garden-stuff, and was not above being thankful to Mrs. Saffery for dripping, broken meat, and even used tea-leaves. Sometimes people who came to look at the cottage gave her sixpence or a shilling for showing it, but such windfalls did not occur very often.

"What a pretty parlour!" cried Edith. "A piano, too!"

"The ceiling is very low," observed Miss Bell, "and the piano has not the additional keys."

"How nice it would be if you would take this cottage, Miss Antony!" said Nessy.

Edith laughed, and said, "I believe it would. Where's the money to come from?"

"I would let it to you very cheap. I wish we could let you have it for nothing."

"Thank you very much; but we cannot leave London, nor afford two sets of lodgings."

Mrs. Early, who had been waiting to speak, now said, wistfully, "No more news of the exploring party, I suppose, miss?"

"None that I have heard of," said Nessy. "I don't think another mail has come in yet."

"You have a son in Australia, have not you?" said Edith. "I have a cousin there. It is such a nice place! He has a pretty farm-house, with a verandah round it, and eleven cows, and twenty pigs."

"Ah! he's a settler," said Mrs. Early, sorrowfully; "but my George has gone into the heart of the undiscovered country to find water, and maybe his bones will bleach in the desert."

"Oh, no! let us hope not," said Edith. "People are very hospitable out there, and directly they hear the crack of a stockman's whip (which may be heard a mile off), they put the kettle on, with a handful or two of tea in it, and cut off two or three dozen mutton-chops and begin to dress them for the travellers that are coming."

Two or three dozen mutton-chops and a

handful of tea did certainly seem very comfortable to Mrs. Early; but she said, after a little pause, " My George mayn't have the luck to come across people like those. My notion of a desert is, that it's all sand and stones."

Miss Antony combatted this notion with the laudable intention of soothing the poor mother's anxieties, which she actually succeeded in doing by sketching and vividly colouring a fancy picture of Australian life, in which, it must be owned, she brought together particulars belonging to widely separate colonies.

At this moment an old man with a milk-can appeared at the gate, and Edith exclaimed—

" Might we not have tea here? How nice it would be ! "

" Oh, yes ! " said Nessy; " and Mrs. Early's kettle is almost boiling, only she has not tea and sugar or bread and butter enough for such a party. Take in some more milk, please, Mrs. Early, and I'll run home for what we want and return directly."

She darted off as she spoke, and Mrs. Early, catching something of the cheerful spirit of the moment, which afforded a variety to her usual sad and still life, bestirred herself to

make the kettle actually boil, which it did not
do yet; and Edith, with the desire of being
useful, took out cups and saucers, and glanced
into the little pantry, where it grieved her to
see little more than Mother Hubbard found
in her cupboard. What were Miss Bell and
Mr. Antony about all this time? Why, Miss
Bell had insisted on Mr. Antony's bringing her
a blue convolvulus without a little black insect
in it, and he was trying to find one, and bringing her one after another that did not answer
the requirement, and there was a good deal of
banter going on between them that came under
the denomination of harmless flirting. At
least, it was harmless enough in its character,
however far from harmless it might be in them,
under any circumstances, to flirt.

"This is how people lived in Arcadia," said
Mr. Antony, at tea-time. "Oh! why is there
now no Arcadia?"

"There *is*," said Nessy; "an inland country
of Peloponnesus." At which the brother and
sister laughed, seemingly at her expense, though
she could not tell why.

"Perhaps I pronounced it wrong," said she,
softly.

"Quite right, Miss Saffery. You are so uncommonly strong in Pinnock's Catechism and Butler's Globes."

"My brother was thinking of an ideal Arcadia," said Edith, "where people had nothing to do but amuse themselves."

"Oh, then he meant the golden age," said Nessy.

It was Nessy's golden age while the brief hour lasted, and then there was a concluding hurry for shawls and parasols, lest they should lose the train. The sun was brightly setting, but it seemed suddenly to cloud to Nessy as she watched the three retreating figures, and then turned indoors very gravely.

"That young lady was very generous to me," said Mrs. Early, showing Nessy two half-crowns. "I dare say she is well off."

"No, I don't know that she is," said Nessy; "but she is very good."

There had been some kind of settlement between Edith and Mrs. Saffery which Nessy had no concern in. But Mrs. Saffery's good word was likewise hers; and Nessy could not but think how much more she liked her than Miss Bell.

Were Mr. Antony and Miss Bell engaged
lovers ?   That was a puzzler to Nessy ; but
Mrs. Saffery decided, without hesitation, that
it was so, and " hoped the young lady had a
good bit of money."

Nessy thought her pluming herself on conscious wealth might help to make her un-
agreeable.   Disagreeable might be too strong
a word.

" A stuck-up young person," Mrs. Saffery
added.   " She looked as if she couldn't say bo
to a goose."

And there the matter dropped.

" I say, mother," began Mr. Saffery, at supper,
suspending, for the moment, his consumption
of bread and cheese, " I'm afraid we're going
to have a bad season.   Here's June nearly
gone and July coming on, and our lodgings
are unlet, and so is the cottage.   I call it a
very bad season."

" Perhaps we had better lock up the cottage,
and pay off Mrs. Early," suggested Mrs. Saffery.

" Oh, I hope not," said Nessy, hastily.

" Why, she doesn't seem to do a bit of good.
She has snug quarters, and perhaps sets people
against the cottage."

“ But people don't go.”

“ Then where's the use of her being there ? ”

This difficult and disagreeable question was solved the next day, or at any rate rendered unnecessary to answer, by a visit from the new curate, Mr. Weir, who, having gone over the cottage, offered to take it for six months, with liberty to continue in possession of it if he wished. “ And I know he can't do better for himself,” afterwards observed Mr. Saffery.

“ Well, there's one load off our minds,” said Mrs. Saffery.

“ I don't think you have any other, have you, mamma ? ” said Nessy.

“ Our lodgings, child.”

“ Oh, to be sure. Only, it's very comfortable to be without people.”

“ Not if they're like Mr. Antony.”

This was too true to be contested.

“ It never rains but it pours.” At least, such is the saying, though, of course, it is not a true one. It expresses the general feeling we have of disappointment, when two eligible things are offered us, and we cannot accept both. About an hour after the arrangement was concluded with Mr. Weir, a widow lady, of prepossessing appearance, entered the post-office, and inquired the terms of Miss Saffery's cottage, saying that Miss Antony had mentioned it to her, and she had come down by the train expressly to see it. It was almost too tantalizing, for the Safferys took a liking to this lady at first sight; and, of course, her being sent by Miss Antony was a voucher for her respectability. How kind of her to think of them!

The lady seemed much disappointed when she found the cottage was let, for she was persuaded it would have suited her, in which case she might have taken it for a permanence. Did they think there was any chance of the other party giving it up, if not very much set upon it? Why, no; because, you see, he was the curate—the new curate, Mr. Weir, who couldn't do better for himself, there being no choice, for there was not another furnished cottage to let in the neighbourhood.

"Ah, yes—yes, indeed," the young widow lady said plaintively, as if it were a very afflicting dispensation, but she must endeavour to submit to it. It was always the way, she said, with anything she set her mind upon: no doubt, it would prove to be for the best.

Would there be any objection, did they think, to her just looking at the cottage? She had a picture of it in her mind's eye, and should like to verify it.

They assured her there could be no objection: Mr. Saffery, chief spokesman, being echoed in everything by his wife, who stood beside him behind the counter; while Nessy stood at the glass-door of the back-parlour, casting wistful glances at the pretty lady with the soft voice and small feet and large dark eyes, so beautifully dressed in the deepest mourning.

" Which is the way? Please give me a very exact direction, for I am so dreadfully stupid—"

" Nessy will show you the way, ma'am, with the greatest of pleasure ; " and Nessy started forward with alacrity, repaid by a speaking smile from those lovely black eyes, without a word spoken.

So Nessy, very much captivated, took her to the cottage ; the interesting stranger conversing with her by the way with much affability, and obtaining, by well-selected inquiries, much local information, both important and unimportant, which she received with many a gentle sigh.

"This is just the place," she observed, after a pause, "to live,—

" 'The world forgetting, by the world forgot.' "

"Dear, do you think so?" said Nessy.

"You don't enter into such feelings, of course," rejoined the lady, with one of her sweet smiles. "Ah, my dear, at *my* time of life, and with *my* bereavements—may you never know what they are!"

Nessy thought this very amiable and touching. "There's the cottage," said she presently.

"Is *that* it?" said her companion, with a little disappointment in her tone. "Well, it *is* pretty, certainly. Yes, very retired and very charming. In fact, just what I wanted. Let me see whether its interior is equally nice."

The front door was a little ajar, so they entered without knock or ring, and crossing the little hall to the dining-room, found Mrs. Early just within it, and—Mr. Weir, on his knees, measuring the carpet with her yard-measure.

His employment naturally made him rather

red in the face, and perhaps he became rather redder when he looked up and saw two female forms in the doorway. He instantly got up.

Nessy thought she had never seen anything prettier or more becoming than her companion's little surprise and the grave dignity with which she bowed, recovered herself, and retreated.

" Pray come in," said Mr. Weir, embarrassed, "if you want to."

It was not a very elegant form of words, and he still held the shabby yellow ribbon in his hand, so that his *abord* altogether was not so prepossessing as the widow lady's, though he undeniably looked like a gentleman. She kept her advantage ; would by no means intrude ; had had no idea any one was in the house but the housekeeper ; had merely intended a visit of curiosity and interest ; and saying this, she re-crossed the threshold.

He followed her with genuine civility, and said, " Pray go over the cottage, if you like it. I have but just taken it, and am measuring the carpet, to see whether a better one of my own will cover it."

But no, she would not—she could not for

the world. She had only heard of it that morning, and being in want of just such a pretty, peaceful retirement, had come down directly to secure it, and found she was just too late. She smiled a little, gave another little inclination, and retraced another step or two.

Mr. Weir's face seemed to say "Well, I'm very sorry for you, but I really cannot give it up." However, what he actually said was, "It was very disappointing."

"Oh," said she, with an expressive look, "I'm *used* to disappointment. 'Tis nothing. Pray think no more of it. *Good* morning."

And this time she really did go; leaving the young curate looking after her in a ruminating manner. When they had quitted the garden, she said absently to Nessy—

"An interesting-looking man. Who is he?"

"Our new curate, Mr. Weir," said Nessy.

Now, before they had started from the post-office, Mrs. Saffery, as a last effort to retain so eligible a party, had said to her, "You wouldn't like these rooms, ma'am, I suppose?" half opening her front-parlour door as she spoke. And the lady had answered by one of her wonderfully expressive looks—"Quite out of the question !"—whereby Mrs. Saffery had felt it *was* quite out of the question, and could only be sorry for it. But now, the fair stranger, after pausing to note one or two points of view on the upland, and pronouncing it, with a regretful sigh, "a pretty, *pretty* place," declared to Nessy she should like to see the lodgings, and judge whether she could by any possibility stuff herself and her belongings into them.

Nessy was agreeably surprised at this, and so was Mrs. Saffery when she learnt it. She did the honours in her most obliging, respectful manner.

" *Very* clean; and very, very small," said the lady. "As for the sofa, oh !" throwing herself for a moment on the hard little couch. "No repose !" Then she looked, considering, around her. "No room for my harp."

" Excuse me, ma'am, I could move this little round table, easy," said Mrs. Saffery, "and an 'arp would stand beautiful in the corner."

" The reverberation would be too powerful," replied the other ; and as Mrs. Saffery was not quite sure what this meant, a pause ensued.

" But, however," cried the lady, suddenly, " I'll try it. "And," with a sweet smile, "the

expense won't be ruinous. You're good creatures, I can see; don't put yourselves in the
least out of the way about me. I have no
whims, I take just what comes: I've known
too much sorrow to be exacting. You'll cook
for me, and—do for me, in short. My tastes
are quite simple; I eat very little—a little
bread and fruit, now and then a chicken; I
suppose the butcher has a sweetbread sometimes? I shall bring my own linen and plate,
not a servant, nothing but my wardrobe, a few
books, and perhaps my harp."

"Is the wardrobe a very heavy one?" said
Mrs. Saffery, doubtfully; "there's an awkward
turn on the stairs."

The lady smiled sweetly, and explained that
the wardrobe simply meant, a box of clothes.

So preliminaries were finally settled.

"And your name, ma'am?"

"Homer. Mrs. Homer."

As Nessy had only heard of Homer the
blind—Pope's Homer—the name struck her as
rather amusing.

CHAPTER XIII.

MRS. HOMER.

HOMER. If you pronounce it slowly, in your most mellifluous voice, you will perceive something soft in it. Ho-mer. It was not a common name. Nessy thought nothing about Mrs. Homer was common. And when Mrs. Saffery had ventured to inquire what part of the world she came from, she had said " Cromer,"—Mrs. Homer, of Cromer, recommended by Miss Antony ;—they were all prepossessed in her favour.

She was not to come down till the following week, having affairs to settle in London, where she was staying at present ; in Cromer Street, Nessy thought, but this was a wild surmise, for Mrs. Homer had not said so. And when Mr. Saffery, who happened to know Cromer Street, remarked that " it was nothing particular of a street," Nessy felt sure she was mistaken.

Though Mrs. Homer was not coming immediately, she was going to send down some of "her things," including the 'arp. And as Mrs. Saffery was not in the general habit of leaving her h's unhasp . . . pshaw! unaspirated, it is to be supposed that owing to some defect in her early education, she happened not to know how harp was spelt, or, at any rate, had forgotten, else why should she say 'arp?—reminding one of the very refined lady who said she liked veal cut with an 'ammy knife!

Meanwhile, Mr. Weir seemed making the most of his time, for he was seen passing from house to house, and cottage to cottage, stooping his tall figure under low doors, and blocking up narrow passages in earnest converse with reluctant housewives. This state of things was particularly observable from the village post-office, which commanded such a wide area; and the Safferys remarked to one another, with some interest, that he seemed a very stirring young gentleman.

In a little while he let them know what the stir was about. He came briskly into the shop, and said—

"Oh, Mrs. Saffery, good morning; I hope

we shall be better friends.   Can I speak a word
to Miss Saffery?"

"Certainly, sir.   Nessy! come down stairs.
Mr. Weir wants to speak to you."

Nessy was touching up her cow—the cow
she had sketched, which Mr. Antony had pronounced "quite a Potter;" but she obeyed the
summons immediately, with a slight expression
of pleasing wonder on her face, which Mr.
Weir thought intelligent.   He began at once
with—

"Oh, good morning, Miss Saffery; you and
I shall, I hope, become better acquainted.   I
want to enlist you on my side."

Nessy looked much pleased, and said, " How,
sir ? "

"I am quite distressed," replied he, "to find
there is no Sunday-school in the place.   During
Mr. Fownes's long illness it has absolutely
dwindled away to nothing.   Since the former
mistress's death no fresh one has been appointed.
I have induced several mothers to promise their
children shall attend, if teachers can be found.
Will you be one of them ?"

"Very gladly, sir, if my mamma will let
me!"

Mrs. Saffery could not, at the instant, decide to say yes or no.

"Mind, I don't say it will be pleasant work to you," said he, quickly. "At first it will be quite the reverse. The children have got out of training; some of them have never had any; at present they are like sheep without a shepherd—sheep going astray, every one his own way. Sheep? I'm afraid you'll find them a good deal more like pigs."

"Your head, Nessy," said Mrs. Saffery, succinctly.

"Her head? what's the matter with her head?" said Mr. Weir. "It's a good, clever-shaped head."

This made them both smile; and Mr. Weir smiled too, thereby disclosing his good white teeth, which gave his face a very pleasant expression.

"Yes, sir, Nessy *is* clever," said Mrs. Saffery, taking up the word. "She's rather what you may call a genius, sir; and was obliged to be took from school, because her faculties were too much for her."

"In what way have these faculties developed themselves ?" inquired he, looking rather amused. "How have they burst out?"

"In the shape of headaches, sir," rejoined Mrs. Saffery; while Nessy felt embarrassed, and fidgetted from one position to another.

"Oh, headaches don't always proceed from overpowering faculties," said the curate. "I have them myself very badly sometimes, but my genius won't set the world on fire. Headaches proceed from various causes—bile, cold, and—"

"Nerves, sir. Nessy's headaches came from nerves."

"Very likely, Mrs. Saffery. Young persons' headaches very often do. Do they unfit you for your daily employments?"

"Oh no, sir! I hardly ever have them now. You know, mamma, I have grown out of them."

"Well, I rather hope you have; only—"

"Of course," said Mr. Weir, "I shall not want to bring on your nervous headaches again. But, if you would not mind trying, I would propose your leaving off directly you found your headache return."

"Thank you, sir. I shall not at all mind trying. I shall like it very much."

"If Mrs. Saffery will be kind enough to let you try—"

"Certainly, sir, certainly," said Mrs. Saffery; "you have made everything so easy by saying she shall leave off if it brings on her headache, that I would not, on any account, make an objection. We have always been steady people, sir, regular church-goers, and Nessy has been well trained, sir."

"Yes, yes, I have no doubt of it; and now I hope she will find pleasure in training others to the same solid advantages she has herself been privileged to obtain. Mrs. Fownes said she was sure she would do so."

"That was very kind of Mrs. Fownes," said mother and daughter, simultaneously.

"Do you know anything of the routine? it is very simple."

"Oh, yes, sir! I've been in the old Sunday-school, but it wasn't quite as nice as it should have been. Mrs. Groat used to hit the children too much."

"There should be no hitting in Sunday-schools," said Mr. Weir. "Pupils should be ruled by the law of kindness."

"Yes, sir; I'm sure that would answer best."

"I never once," joined in Mrs. Saffery, emulous of the clergyman's approbation, "I never once raised my hand against Nessy, sir —no, never, except in the way of washing and brushing."

"And you have been repaid in the affection of a good daughter," said he, looking kindly from one to the other, and making their hearts swell as they exchanged glances. "Well, Miss Saffery, I shall start you off on Sunday morning, and you will have the reins completely in your own hands at first, at all events, for I have not yet enlisted another teacher—every one seems afraid, or idle, or uninterested."

"Please, sir, I should like it all the better in my own hands. I could work out my own plans."

"Have you any? Come, that's capital. I see, you and I shall be great friends." And he cordially shook hands with her, she and her mother equally proud and pleased.

"I shall look in again on you before Sunday," said he; "but I must go now, for time fails me. Halloa! what is coming in here? Not a coffin, surely?"

"Oh, it's the 'arp!" cried Mrs. Saffery, as

a railway-porter appeared at the door with a cumbrous package on his back.

"The what?" said Mr. Weir, in surprise.

"Mrs. Homer's harp, sir," explained Nessy.

"Mrs. Homer?" he repeated. "I have not that name down. Is she of this parish?"

"No, sir; she has just taken our lodgings. She comes from Cromer Street, or Cromer."

"Mrs. Homer, of Cromer," repeated he, smiling. "I must look her up when I've time. Perhaps I shall make her useful, or get her to subscribe. Is she old or young?"

"The lady, sir, whom I brought to your cottage."

"O—h!" and his tone quite changed as he made this very long Oh. "So *that* was Mrs. Homer, of Cromer. Ah! Well, I hope she will do some good among us. She was disappointed at not getting the cottage. So she plays the harp—King David played the harp. Good morning!" and he briskly walked off.

In truth, they were rather glad to get rid of him, for he blocked up the doorway, while the railway-porter stood, the picture of patience, with "the harp, his sole remaining joy," on his back. Its exterior covering was a very dirty old sacking, under which was a dirty old blanket; but under these peeped out a very smart stamped leather case, which impressed Mrs. Saffery and Nessy with profound respect for the stringed instrument it contained. Moreover, that it did actually contain aforesaid instrument was evidenced by a certain twangle or groan of suffering emitted from its innermost depths when the porter, with more concern for himself than the 'arp, bumped it down in the corner. He objected to depart without being paid, so Mrs. Saffery produced the money while Nessy signed the book. Then mother and daughter contemplated the dirty sacking a little, longing, but not presuming, to remove it; and Mrs. Saffery curiously examined the direction-card, superscribed in a very pretty, lady-like hand, and having, on the off side, "Mrs. Homer" engraved in old English characters, with no address annexed. Then they began to say to one another what a very nice gentleman Mr. Weir was, how bent he seemed on doing good, how conciliating his manners were, how pleasant his voice was, and how gratifying it would be to assist him in any way. Nessy did not return to her cow, but began to mend her father's stockings with great zeal. It was an employment she was particularly fond of whenever she had anything interesting to think about; and that was the case now. She had often had a vague wish to do good, but saw no opening for it, and here was one expressly presented to her. Ragged children immediately acquired a value in her eyes which they had never had before. She resolved to make them clean and make them good. Her primary notion was to teach them as she would have liked to be taught herself.

With her head full of philanthropic schemes, Nessy's dreamings were much more profitable than usual; and though they now and then diverged to the Antonys and the new lodger, they soon returned to the Sunday-school.

"I will teach them till they are tired," thought she, "and then tell them a story."

What should she teach them? What should the story be? Here were new ranges of thought.

Mr. Weir brought a handful of letters for the second post, and came in to buy some stamps. It was a pleasure to Nessy to serve him.

" I must go away on Monday," said he, " but
I hope to give you a fair start on Sunday.
There will probably be two dozen or more
children. You must begin from the first, with
marks. One mark for early attendance in the
morning, one for the same in the afternoon,
one for lessons well said, and one for good
conduct during the day. I must try to find
time to supply you with little tickets, with the
number and date written on them, just as
vouchers to encourage the parents."

" That will trouble you, sir. I will gladly
make them."

" Will you ? Do, then. You and I shall
work well together, I see. You must enter the
marks in a class-book, which I will supply you
with ; and at the end of the year they will be
counted up, and the children will have a penny
a dozen for them. This they will add to their
shoe-club, or have the value in little books—
hymn-books, and so forth. You look dissentient ; what is your objection ? "

" I think they would like the money itself
so very much better, sir. It would be so much
more of an object to them to work for money
of their very own."

"Do you think so?   Why, they would spend it in lollipops!   It would do them no good."

"The earning it would do them good, sir; and perhaps they would not spend it in lollipops; not all of them, at least."

It was he who looked dissentient this time.

"What makes you think they would like the money best?"

"I know the feeling, sir."

He laughed. "Oh, come, that's a cogent reason."

"We all like laying out money of our own accord, sir, or having the privilege of saving it."

"Of being free agents, in fact. Well, I believe we do. But some of these little tots are hardly fit to be free agents. I scarcely know what to say to it. It will all go in gingerbread, you'll see."

"I might influence them, sir."

"Well, we'll think about it, Miss Saffery. Influence them as much as you can, by all means. There will be little prizes, you know, besides, and a Christmas tea-party to the children whose names have not once been in the black book. Powerful allurements!"

"Yes, sir."

"It has been said that the *teacher* is the school. As is the teacher, such is the school. An intelligent teacher will have intelligent scholars. A pious teacher will make pious scholars. You see this? you feel this?"

"Yes, sir."

"But a teacher who is *not* pious, is *not* intelligent, mind you, is no good. I am not speaking of extensive book-learning, but of plain, practical wisdom; the heart-knowledge of the best of books. As far as you have this, you will do good; if you have it not, you can do *no* real good. Do you see this? do you feel it?"

"Yes, sir" (very seriously).

"I am sure you do. To teach others, even little children, you must constantly be teaching yourself; renewing your knowlege, increasing your knowledge. To teach yourself (lowering his voice and speaking very earnestly), you must be taught of God. You must be taught by His Spirit. You know how to seek it, how to obtain it—by prayer. You must be teachable as a little child. And then you will be able to teach little children."

He shook hands with her across the counter, and was gone. A third person was present, whom he had not noticed. Mrs. Saffery, coming in while they were talking, had fidgeted a little at first, to attract his attention ; but, on second thoughts, she preferred being without it, and stood listening. When he turned to go, she remained in the background. Then she said—

"Nessy, that is a good young man :" and her mouth twitched.

As for Nessy, she ran up to her little bed-room, and shut herself in.

" By-the-bye," said Mr. Saffery, the next time they assembled at meal-time, "what's going to become of Mrs. Early ? "

" Ah, I thought of that," said Nessy, "and would have asked Mr. Weir, only he was talking of things so much more interesting, that I did not like to interrupt him."

"Take my word for it, Nessy," said her mother, "that Mr. Weir is one of those people who, the seldomer you interrupt, the better. He puts me somewhat in mind of the girl in the fairy fable who never opened her mouth but there fell out a pearl, a diamond, and a flower."

"That's a pretty idea of yours, Betsy," said Mr. Saffery. "I never saw any good in the story before."

"Oh, as for pretty ideas," said she, pleased at his praise and his calling her Betsy, "I leave them to Nessy and Mr. Weir."

"But, about Mrs. Early," said Nessy. "Shall I look in on her?"

"Yes, do; and if Mr. Weir's servants are coming in, she can step down here as soon as she's discharged, and I'll settle with her."

So Nessy took the earliest opportunity of paying her visit of inquiry. She found the tall old man, whom Mr. Antony had painted, at work in the front garden. He looked very happy, and said he had told Mr. Weir he wasn't good for much, but was good for a little, and Mr. Weir had told him to come and go, and do a little when he was able, and leave off when he wasn't, and he would pay him what was reason.

"He's a kind gentleman to be under," said he, "and this is a pretty bit of ground, as has always hit my fancy; and now the weather's not remarkable hot, I shall get it all into condition by degrees, as you'll see. There's a lot of rubbish in yonder corner as didn't ought never to have been left there all this time, and will burn finely and make first-rate manure, that I shall dig well in. I can dig with my left foot, though the other's past service."

"Take care you don't burn down the laurel hedge," said Nessy.

He gave her a knowing smile, and said—

"Trust me for that; I wasn't born yesterday."

Mrs. Early, usually so pitiful, received her with smiles.

"I'm not going away, Miss Saffery," said she. "Mr. Weir wants a second servant—his London cook doesn't like the country, though one would have supposed it an agreeable change after Shoreditch, but there's no accounting for tastes—and so he has requested me to be his housekeeper; at any rate, till Mrs. Weir comes down and sees need to make any alteration."

"Is Mr. Weir married, then?" said Nessy, in surprise.

"Oh, no, it's his mother; an elderly lady. He's the only son of his mother, and she is a widow. Those were his very own words; at least, Scripture words that he saw fit to make use of. I told him it was exactly my own case; that George was my only son, and I was a widow; not an importunate widow, I hoped, but an indigent one, as everybody knew: and though I had never expected to go out to service in my old age, yet I had been getting downwards by little and little, never getting the remittances my poor boy had talked of sending me; so that it was an object to me, a great object, to be provided for, and if he'd only try me, he'd find I could save him many a penny. The cleaning isn't heavy, and I can cook a cutlet pretty well when I've a cutlet to cook. So I hope I shall suit him, for I'm sure he'll suit me. But he goes to London o' Monday."

Nessy's spare time after supper was spent in making the tickets.

CHAPTER XIV.

SUNDAY WELL SPENT.

SUNDAY witnessed a decided success. Nessy was at her post at half-past nine, and was soon followed by a rabble of youngsters, who clattered boisterously in, as if the prime object was to see how much noise they could make. She knew every one of them by name, and, with a sudden inspiration of genius, began shaking hands with them all round, in this way :—

"Mary, how do you do?—why, how nice you have made yourself look! Stand here, please. Joseph, how do *you* do? I'm glad you're come. Stand on *this* side, please. How do you do, Patty?—stand next Mary, please. I shall soon have you all sorted. Philip, how do you do?—you shall stand next to Joseph. Mr. Weir will be in presently. I want to get you all in order before he comes. Janet, how do you do ?—stand here, please," &c. &c. &c. The cheerful, kind, but rather subdued tones of her voice produced a general lull, till broken by a giggle from the youngest ; on which Nessy gave an exculpatory look at the rest, as much as to say, " She's very little—we must forgive her." The boys, meanwhile, stood kicking their heels, awkwardly enough, and seemed meditating a scrimmage.

" Mr. Weir is going to open the school presently," resumed Nessy; " and meanwhile I will tell you something you will perhaps like to know. Come a little nearer—no, not quite so near. Yes, that will just do. You will begin, from the first, with marks. Every one who comes in good time on Sunday mornings will get a good mark. You were all in good time— You will all have a good mark."

" Tom Brown hasn't come," one of the little little boys burst out. " He won't get a good mark."

" All the worse for Tom Brown. Perhaps he is not well. If you come in good time in the afternoon, you will get another good mark. If you say all your lessons well, you will get another good mark. That's three ! For general good conduct, you'll get another good mark. That's four!"

"What's general good conduct?" said Joseph.

Nessy paused, and then said, "Being orderly and obedient. Not speaking too loud. Being polite to one another" ("Oh, my!" in a whisper) "and kind to the little ones. Going to church, and behaving well there; and—being good in general."

This was received in silence. "All the marks will be set down in a book, and you will have little tickets besides, to carry home. *That* will please father and mother. And at Christmas all the good marks will be counted up, and you will get a penny a dozen; and prizes and a tea-party besides."

"Hurray!" said Philip.

"And now let us kneel down, and say the Lord's Prayer."

Down knelt the girls; and, with a little shuffling, scuffling, and pushing, down knelt the boys; and their voices followed Nessy's with one accord. At this propitious moment, Mr. Weir entered, and stood for an instant in pleased surprise; then knelt down too, and added a strong " Amen !" and the benediction. The children rose, completely sobered, and then he arranged a few preliminaries, gave Nessy the class-book, took the boys under his own teaching, while she took the girls ; and soon, as orderly, well-organized a little school was in full occupation as a benevolent teacher would wish to see.

When the church bells began to ring, Nessy rose and said, "Now I must go home, to go to church with my father ; and I hope you will go too, and behave very nicely, and get good-conduct marks in the afternoon. I am so glad we have made such a nice beginning. Mind you come again in good time. Good-bye."

"Cannot you accompany them to church, Miss Saffery ? " said Mr. Weir, coming up to her.

"No, sir. My father would miss me. I think they will be very good. They look as if they would. You will, won't you ? "

"Yes," cried some of them.

"Suppose we finish with a hymn ; with one verse of a hymn," said Mr. Weir ; and he led the doxology.

Nessy entertained and interested her father on their way to church with an account of their proceedings; and he was pleased at her taking so prominent a part, especially as it had not hindered her being his companion. He and Mrs. Saffery took it in turns to keep house, and he would not have liked to go to church alone.

Mr. Weir preached on "The poor ye have always with you;" and he observed that there were degrees of comparison between the poor, so that even the very poor could find those yet poorer, towards whom they could always exercise compassion—if not with money, with sympathy, assistance, and loving words. He spoke of the London poor, and their want of many things that even the poorest in country places scarcely knew the want of—want of light, of air, of drinkable water, of a drop of milk. He spoke of those "whose pity gave ere charity began"—whose instinctive compassion, that is, made them hasten to relieve, before charity, strictly speaking, had had time to operate; and he enforced compassion by reminding his hearers of what we all owed to a compassionate God.

It was preaching that none could sleep under; that the very poor listened to with as deep attention as their richer neighbours.

"And how did you like Mr. Weir to-day,

Saffery ? " said Mrs. Saffery, as they sat at dinner.

" I wish more could have heard him," said Mr. Saffery. " It was what I may call an anecdotical sermon."

" Hum !—that sounds odd," said his wife.

" Odd or even, so it was. He gave us instances and cases . . . you might have heard a pin drop."

" Cases like what ? "

" Well, he told us of a poor woman in Shoreditch, talking to him about her soul, and while they were talking, two little starving children kept plucking her apron and clamouring for food. She took part of a carrot out of her pocket, cut them each a slice off it, and put it in her pocket again. She had picked the carrot out of the gutter. It was all the food she had in the house."

" Tell mother about the old gentleman, father," said Nessy.

" He spoke of an old gentleman, from personal knowledge, who had given away twenty thousand pounds in acts of benevolence, and lived himself on a hundred and seventy pounds a year."

"Well, if Mr. Weir can tell things like that in his sermons," said Mrs. Saffery, "I expect he'll have plenty of listeners."

"I'll be bound to say," added Mr. Saffery, "that there was more substance in the sermon we heard this morning, than in all the sermons Dr. Fownes has preached in the whole course of his life."

"That's a good deal to say, too, Saffery."

"I say it, though, and I mean it."

The afternoon school was almost as satisfactory as the morning, though a few boys absented themselves. All had good-conduct marks. They began and ended with singing hymns; and they had Scripture questions, and a little reading, and Nessy read them a short story.

She felt at night that it had not been a day of rest to her, but a very happy day. Mr. Weir had lent her a very interesting book; it was "Mendip Annals;" and as she read it by snatches during the week, the doings of the brave-hearted Patty More fired her with generous emulation.

Mr. Weir was gone, and Mrs. Homer was coming; so no more reading, at present, for

Nessy. Mrs. Homer came down on Saturday afternoon, looking as pensive and sweetly pretty as before, and the railway porter brought her luggage on his barrow. Mrs. Saffery was rather put out at her not having written to tell her what to provide for her Sunday dinner, or whether she would want to dine on her arrival. Mrs. Homer smiled sweetly, and said it was not of the least consequence, she was never very hungry, and had had some bread and butter; she could wait very well for tea.

Would she like something with her tea?

" A little fruit."

Mrs. Saffery did not know of any fruit but apples.

Apples were smiled at, silently. " Prawns?"

Mrs. Saffery, dismayed, assured her there were no prawns. Would she have a chop?

Head shaken. " Oh, it did not at all signify. She never minded."

Would she like an egg?

Well, yes, she thought eggs would do—they were very simple. Or a little preserve. Either. She never cared.

What would she like for to-morrow?

Oh, anything there was. A chicken, a rabbit,

a little bit of fish, a slice of their own hot joint. She left it entirely to Mrs. Saffery.

"Fish on a Sunday!" muttered Mrs. Saffery, as she returned to her own quarters: "where can this lady have lived? Oh, at Cromer, to be sure, where you might catch fish, perhaps, from your parlour window. And we've nothing but a beefsteak pie. I don't suppose she'll touch that. Do ask her, Nessy, when you go up, whether she will have pie or a chicken. Get yes or no from her, if you can. I hate yea-and-nay persons that don't care, and leave it to you, and end by fixing on the most unaccountable things. In an inland place like this, one never gets fish, unless from London; though a man comes round, indeed, once in a way, with herrings and mackerel."

Here the bell rang violently, and Nessy flew up stairs to answer it. Mrs. Homer was in her bedroom on her knees before a trunk.

"Did I make that abominable noise?" said she, sweetly. "I had no idea the bell would ring so easily. Do forgive me."

Nessy assured her there was nothing to forgive.

"I cannot untie this cord. The knot is so

tight, it will break my nails. Is there a man in the house ? "

"My papa is out," said Nessy; "but I daresay I can do it."

"Oh, I don't like to ask you. The porter should have done it. So stupid not to ask him." (All this while Nessy was at work, tooth and nail.) "There! you've broken *your* nail now. Does it bleed? will you have my nail-scissors? Please, don't strain yourself. The box may just as well remain where it is till the morning."

"But to-morrow is Sunday," suggested Nessy, "and you may stumble over it if it is left here."

"Ah, then, to-morrow being Sunday, I must unpack it for my books. One depends so on a book on Sunday."

Nessy, learning the contents of the box, tugged at the cord with the more zeal, and at length got it off. Then there was a hunt for the key. It could not be found; but Mrs. Homer said she did not mind.

"My mamma desired me to ask," said Nessy, "whether you would like beefsteak pie for dinner to-morrow, or——"

"Oh, I should like beefsteak pie, of all things!"

This was quite a relief; but when Mrs. Homer added that she should prefer dining after the second service, Nessy was in trouble, for this would involve the whole family's dining late too, which she knew her father would not consent to. So she had to make an embarrassed explanation; but Mrs. Homer set all to rights by assuring her that it did not in the least signify, she did not mind.

"When one visits Arcadia," said she, "one must do as the Arcadians do."

Nessy thought this a lovely metaphor, and went down stairs quite pleased.

"She is certainly very sweet-tempered, mamma," said she, "for she accommodated herself to our hours directly."

"All the better for both parties," said Mrs. Saffery. "Take out a pot of black currant jam, Nessy. I have boiled her two eggs, so she can have her choice."

Mrs. Homer's choice was something like Nelson's coxswain's, for she disposed of it all, in such a sentimental, meditative way, that she seemed eating in a fit of absence. "You need not wait," said she sweetly to Nessy; "I can't bear to trouble you."

So, though Nessy could truly have said the trouble was a pleasure, she did as she was bid, shut the door after her, and never was chid. And when she cleared the table, there remained on it two empty egg-shells, an empty bread-and-butter plate, and empty jelly-pot.

"Well, that young lady *was* hungry," Mrs. Saffery observed, smiling.

Mrs. Homer found the key of her book-box, and spent some hours in unpacking it and arranging her clothes.

"Do go and ask her, Nessy, for the sheets and spoons," said Mrs. Saffery. "It's no good keeping up this nice airing-fire till midnight. Your father wants to be in bed."

Then want must be his master, or he must go to bed some hours before the rest of his family, for Mrs. Homer remained reading a book she had opened, as she sat on the floor, till it was too dark to see, and then she rang for lights, and reclined on the couch that had "no repose" till between eleven and twelve o'clock.

"That young lady must have got an exciting book, seemingly," said Mrs. Saffery.

"I don't think she has a book," said Nessy. "She did not bring one down."

"Whatever is she doing, then?"

"Thinking, I believe," said Nessy.

"Thinking!" exclaimed Mr. Saffery. "Really, that's too bad. I shall go to Bedfordshire." And he proceeded to shut the shutters with much clangour.

"Do go and ask her, Nessy, if she'll take anything," said Mrs. Saffery, losing patience.

"Bid her take my advice, and take herself to bed," said Mr. Saffery, softly.

The answer, in a drowsy voice, to Nessy's inquiry, was—

"Nothing, thank you, Thomas."

"Ma'am?" said Nessy.

"Dear me, I believe I have been dozing," said Mrs. Homer. "What a thief there is in the candle! Is it bed-time?"

"It is rather past *our* usual bedtime, ma'am. Nearly twelve o'clock."

"Ah, well," said she, rising and twinkling her eyelids. "I must learn Arcadian hours. All 'beauty sleep,' you know, is before twelve o'clock."

And smiling good-night at Nessy, she took

up a bedroom candle and went towards the door.

"What o'clock shall I call you, ma'am?"

"Oh, to-morrow is Sunday. Say, nine o'clock."

Nine o'clock? and the Sunday school was to open at half-past! Arcadian hours, indeed!

When Nessy, with very lengthened face, told her mother what orders she had received, Mrs. Saffery said, with great resolution,—

"It don't signify, Nessy. I'm not going to have my household rules and regulations upset for any stranger, however die-away and pretty she may be. Duties is duties; and you having pledged yourself, as one may say, to stick by the school till Mr. Weir came back, stick to it you must. So you'll just breakfast on bread and milk to-morrow, and be off to the children, and I'll wait on Mrs. Homer."

"Thank you, mother!"

"I wonder," said Mr. Saffery, with a gleam of mischief in his sleepy eyes, "whether the lady will be disturbed by the mail-bag in the middle of the night."

But no! though the guard thumped and thundered as usual, Mrs. Homer slept the sleep

of an Arcadian, and never turned on her pillow.　Nor, till—

> "Lapdogs give themselves the rousing shake
> Did the sleepless lady just at twelve awake ;—"

and found it wanted only an hour to dinner.
She said "it would be a farce to get breakfast
for her—she would just have a draught of new
milk and a biscuit."

New milk, of course, was not within reach
at that hour, nor had Mrs. Saffery any biscuits
but twelve-a-penny, which Nessy had bought
for the tiniest of her pupils.　However, Mrs.
Homer said it did not in the least signify ; and
she dressed very leisurely, and strolled round
the little garden with a parasol, and, one way
and another, killed time till people came out of
church.

It must here be mentioned, rather too late,
that on the previous evening, while unpacking
her books, Mrs. Homer, on coming to her
prayer-book, had said carelessly to Nessy—

"Does that young clergyman—Mr. Weir, I
think you call him—preach to-morrow morning ? "

"No, ma'am," said Nessy, "he is away at
present ;" on hearing which, Mrs. Homer looked

rather blank. It may therefore be conjectured that, if she had heard he would officiate, she might so far have overcome her torpor as to get up in time for church; but this must be one of those questions which are to remain for ever unsolved.

When honest Mr. Saffery, with shining face and erect head, marched churchwards with Nessy at his side, he said—

"Your mother has lost her turn this morning, owing to our curiosity of a lodger, in spite of her providing a meat pie that I might have no trouble about dinner. However, what's her loss is my gain, though we shan't have Mr. Weir : I don't forget what he said last Sunday, that church is not the parson's house, but the house of God."

Nessy's character was now rapidly developing under the force of circumstances, though they were of the simplest kind; and when she waited on Mrs. Homer at dinner, there was such animation in her happy face, that it attracted that lady's notice, and she said—

"You look very bright, Miss Saffery."

"I feel very bright, ma'am," said Nessy. "I have had such a happy morning."

"What has tended to make it so?"

"Going to the Sunday-school, ma'am, which I had all to myself, in Mr. Weir's absence."

"Dear me, that must have been very arduous."

"It was rather so, but the children were very good."

"It must be stupid work, surely, to be a teacher in a Sunday-school. You can scarcely have a day of rest."

"It does interfere with absolute rest, certainly," said Nessy; "but I hope it is not, therefore, breaking God's commandment, since it is doing His work. You know our Saviour Himself decided that we might do good on the Sabbath day."

"Ah, yes—yes, indeed," said Mrs. Homer.

By way of doing good on the Sabbath day, Mrs. Homer afterwards strayed to a warm, sheltered bank, embowered in ivy, where she enjoyed the *dolce far niente,* and occasionally turned the leaves of a little gilt-edged volume, bound in pink watered silk, called "Sighs for Every Day in the Week," by Clementillo Sospiroso.

CHAPTER XV.

SACRED MUSIC.

TOWARDS dusk Mrs. Homer found a Sabbath-evening employment for herself. The Safferys were sitting meditatively together, expecting her to ring for candles, and Mr. Saffery was dozing a little, when all at once they heard a subdued sound like this—

Twing! Twing! Twing!

" Why, goodness, if she hasn't gone and un-packed her 'arp of a Sunday!" cried Mrs. Saffery. "What would Mr. Weir say to that, I wonder?"

"Mr. Weir said King David played the harp," said Nessy.

"That doesn't sound to me," said Mr. Saffery, waking up, "one of Mr. Weir's profoundest observations."

This solo was followed by its symphony—

Twing—twing—twing—

and then the music ceased.

"Come, she hasn't given us much of it,"
said Mrs. Saffery, after a pause, "and an 'arp
is a sacred species of music."

"I like the tone," said Nessy.

"Yes," said Mr. Saffery, "it makes a kind of
rumbustion in the atmosphere, that you can
feel as well as hear. I wonder if the lady is a
Roman Car-tholic."

"If I found she was," said Mrs. Saffery,
"away she should go. I don't want any pro-
verts in *my* house. Have you seen any cruci-
fixes or images about the rooms, Nessy?"

"No, mamma. Oh, I don't think there's any
danger. She seemed to wish to hear Mr. Weir."

"Mr. Weir, if he has a mind to, may do her
a mint of good," said Mrs. Saffery. Then, after
a little thought, "If this lady, now, would give
you a few lessons on the 'arp, as Mr. Antony
did in painting, you'd be a finished young
lady."

Nessy turned quite red at the thought.

"Oh, mamma, don't think of it!" said she,
imploringly.

"Why not? Mrs. Homer is not superior in
her line to Mr. Antony in his, I fancy; so why
should she be above it?"

"Mr. Antony was glad of a little ready-money."

"And why shouldn't Mrs. Homer be?"

"No, my dear, no; you've no reason to suspect that," said Mr. Saffery. "Time enough for that when she doesn't pay her bills."

"I'm certain I could never bear to play the harp," said Nessy. "Drawing is a nice, quiet employment, and may be carried on out of sight, but music can never be practised out of hearing."

"Well, and if people do hear?"

"Oh, I couldn't bear it! I don't know that I've any ear."

"You've a pretty little pipe of your own," said Mr. Saffery. "I thought so this morning when you were warbling beside me."

"I don't know that I've any finger."

"There *may* be something in that," rejoined he, reflectively. "A great deal is required of the little finger in harp-playing, or else nothing at all—I forget exactly which. Your fingers may not be adaptuated to instrumentation. I've heard tell of people whose fingers were all thumbs."

"But if Mrs. Homer were to look at her

fingers," insisted Mrs. Saffery, "she would know directly whether they would do for fingering."

"Well, my dear, we hardly know how Mrs. Homer herself plays yet."

This struck Mrs. Saffery with the force of truth. At the same instant the bell rang, and Nessy, taking the liberty of guessing what it rang for, carried in candles. In doing so she tripped over the old sacking and blanket that lay in a heap just inside the parlour-door, and the candles nearly alighted in Mrs. Homer's lap. As soon as this was apologised for and forgiven, Mrs. Homer expressed a wish to see Mr. Saffery. Nessy, having carried off the wraps, told him. Never was man more surprised.

"Want to see *me*?" said he, turning red, and settling his shirt-collar a little. "Are you sure she didn't mean your mother?"

"Quite sure," said Nessy.

"She must have something to complain of," said he, rather uneasily, adding to himself, "I'm sure I hope she hasn't heard our little remarks."

It required all the force of character he possessed to enter the lady's presence without visible trepidation. She had placed the two

candles on the chimneypiece before the little
looking-glass, so that he said afterwards they
were equal to the light of four, and it seemed
exactly like going into company.

"Don't shut the door, Nessy," said Mrs.
Saffery, in a loud whisper; "it's as much as
my virtue is equal to, not to make use of the
keyhole."

"Do you ever drive, Mr. Saffery?" said
Mrs. Homer, sweetly.

"*Drive*, ma'am?" repeated he, at his wit's
end.

"Yes—a little pony-carriage of any kind."

"Never, ma'am, never! I'm not the least
of a whip. When I married Mrs. Saffery, I
drove her in a one-horse shay and spilt her."

"Dear me! what a mercy she was preserved! But is there anything of the kind
to let here by the day or hour?"

"No doubt, ma'am, though hacks are not
much in request here, because, you see, the
real gentry keep their own carriages, and the
gentry that—in short, there's no great choice;
but, certainly, there's a little basket-carriage
at the Swan, only its near-wheel is mostly off."

"That's dangerous, is not it?"

“Well, ma’am, if it did come down, you wouldn’t fall far; and the pony’d be right glad to stand still directly you said ‘ Woe ! ’ ”

“Well, then, I think I might try that. I want to see the environs.”

“The what, ma’am ? ”

“The neighbourhood. I suppose you have some pretty drives, green lanes, glimpses of country-seats, and so forth ? ”

“Yes, ma’am, yes, to be sure,” answered he, briskly. And, opening so unexpectedly on a subject with which he was perfectly familiar, he talked rapidly and with great pleasure to himself, to the satisfaction of his lodger and the amusement and curiosity of Mrs. Saffery, who could only catch a word now and then. He returned with a broad smile on his face.

“Well,” said he, after cautiously shutting the door, “she’s a nice, pleasant-spoken lady, when you come to know a little of her, that’s a fact.”

“You’re captivated, Saffery, *that’s* the fact.”

“Stuff ! She’s a very fine woman, though ; and what with the instrument and the lights, and all together, I hardly knew the parlour.”

“Well, what was it all about ? ”

"She wants to hire a carriage and explore the neighbourhood, and she asked about the drives; so I told her of a few—that was all. Nessy, it's getting late, and I'm growing sleepy."

Presently Mrs. Homer's bell rang again. After a little delay Nessy answered it.

"Were you reading aloud?"

"Family prayers, ma'am."

"You seem to be very good people—*very* good. Well, I shall not want anything more to-night. It's getting late, isn't it?—Only half-past nine? Well, I shall have the more beauty-sleep."

At half-past ten next morning the little basket-carriage stood at the door, and Mrs. Homer presently stepped into it. Mrs. Saffery had implored her either to expressly order her dinners herself, or to give her authority to provide for her; on which she said—

"Well, then, let me have a plain mutton-cutlet, with tomato-sauce; and a simple rice-pudding, flavoured with vanille."

"But, dear me! where shall I get the tomatos and vanille?" said Mrs. Saffery.

"O, never mind. I don't in the least care.

I'm never very hungry. A slice of bread-and-butter, whenever I come in. What are you going to have yourselves?"

"Nothing you could touch, ma'am, I'm sure! Just what is in house, and a few sprats."

"Sprats! how very amusing. I should like to try them, by all means. I don't know the taste of a sprat. Are they dear?"

"Goodness me, no, ma'am! You may get them, sometimes, sixty a penny."

"Oh, how amusing. Do buy me a pennyworth. I shall not want more than six. You may have the rest yourselves."

"Oh, ma'am, you may have some of ours, and welcome; we shall never miss them. And I'll provide the cutlet and pudding too, only I'm afraid you can't have vanille."

The little boy jerked the pony's rein as she spoke, and the rejoinder jerked out of Mrs. Homer's roseate lips was, "Never mind!"

She was absent some hours, and came home delighted with her drive, and with the pretty, *pretty* places she had seen—but with a fearful headache; a headache that prevented her reckoning up the money she owed for the carriage with anything like accuracy; and, then, as she half whispered across the counter,

"How much was she to give—Lubin?"

"What you please, ma'am," said Mr. Saffery, when he understood what she meant.

"Will fourpence be enough?   Sixpence?"

"Well, ma'am, these boys get spoilt by the gentry.   I believe a shilling will be nearer the mark, considering you've been out all the morning."

And Lubin did not seem at all overpowered by the munificence of the benefaction.   Indeed, Mrs. Homer had certainly had her shilling's-worth for her shilling, for she had extracted a surprising amount of information from him concerning the people and affairs of the neigh-bourhood.   Yet every inquiry was so plaintive, that she never gave the least idea of a gossip. During dinner she told Nessy a little of where she had been, what she had seen, and what she had learnt, so placidly and pleasantly, that Nessy was more than ever impressed in her favour. Placidity was the order of the evening; Mrs. Homer was completely tired, and was just in the condition to enjoy a book on the couch which yielded no repose.　And the book was a sensation novel.

"I believe she wants to settle among us," said Nessy to her parents.

"Why, isn't she settled among us already?"

"No; she says this would never do for a permanence; she wants more accommodation, more space.　Not that she wants to receive her friends, for her passion is solitude; but she would like a place where she *could* receive them suitably, if she wished."

"Nessy, you talk like a printed book!"

"I remember her exact words, because I thought she expressed herself so nicely."

"She *does* express herself nicely," said Mr. Saffery, with decision.　"She's quite the gentle-woman."

"I wonder how long she has been a widow," said Mrs. Saffery.　"I wonder what her husband was."

By the end of the week they all seemed to understand each other, and they got on very comfortably, though Mrs. Saffery's indirect questions and feelers had not thrown any light on Mrs. Homer's antecedents.　When she said—

"So young a lady as you, ma'am, must have suffered much, to be so early widowed."

She was checked at once with—

"Excuse me; there are some subjects so tender, that it is best not to enter on them."

And this was said so sweetly and plaintively, that Mrs. Saffery felt herself a grievous sinner for having wounded her, though there were no tears in the soft eyes under the drooping eye-lids.

As for the harp, it was not much heard. It took so much tuning, that by the time it was tuned, the tuner was tired; and then the cover was put on again. Nor was it a great beauty; it was a small, single-actioned harp, very old-fashioned and tarnished; so that it was more ornamental in its handsome cover than out of it. Its tone, however, was very good; it had a good sounding-board, partly because it was old and the varnish was covered with an in-finity of small cracks, through which the sound oozed. Again, Mrs. Homer kept it very loosely strung, as the wandering harpers do who go about the streets, both to save the strings from breaking, and because it was much easier to sing to a harp considerably under concert pitch. Mrs. Homer, however, said she "never sang now."

Mrs. Saffery had less trouble now in the commissariat department, because, as she said, she had found that, though Mrs. Homer was much given to ask for extraor'nary things, she was quite content with what was or'nary; especially with a little garnish. She really was, as she had declared herself, easy to please when it came to the point; and though she frequently had the air of having much to complain of, she never complained; was never scorney.

Though she said she considered her lodging "only a temporary little lodge in the wilderness," yet this little lodge was now considerably embellished by the hand of taste. Some very pretty tablecovers, mats, penwipers, and little ornaments were produced from her stores; the muslin curtain was better hung; fresh flowers were introduced in profusion; an Affghan blanket in process of knitting formed a gorgeous bit of colour on the couch; and a globe with two gold fish gleamed in the sun. All these little elegances took up much of Mrs. Homer's time; she was evidently fonder of arranging and re-arranging them, than of reading, working, or writing. Her stock of books was not very ample, after all; it comprised gaily-bound volumes of engravings, landscape annuals, and poems, which were laid out in due form on the table, and a good many works of fiction, French and English, too unornamental to be brought down stairs till after dark.

One day she made preparations in great state for colouring a sketch, but, after getting her paints ready, and talking very artistically to Nessy, she discovered that she should like a walk, and the paint-box was closed. She now dined at a little side-table, that her books and knick-knacks might not be disturbed; but the word "dinner" was tabooed. "She didn't dine, she never cared for dinner; she lunched at one, and had tea and a little fruit at six." Fruit was generally represented by a roasted apple, and sometimes by a baked apple dumpling. "*What's* in a name?" why, a good deal, we all know.

One day, when, to give some order to Mrs. Saffery, she stepped into the back-parlour, she saw a little sketch on the table, and said in surprise—

"That's very nicely done—who did it?"

"Our Nessy, ma'am," said Mrs. Saffery, much gratified; "she's a great one for her pencil."

"What a nice touch she has! Dear me, how curious that she should have such a talent. So quiet about it, too! I never had the least idea. —Self-taught?"

"No, ma'am; she had the best of teaching— from Mr. Antony."

"Mr. Antony! Dear me; did he condescend to give her lessons? I should never have supposed it."

"Mr. Antony, ma'am, is above giving lessons as a general rule; he objected at first, but he saw Nessy had talent—genius, indeed, he called it—and so we came to an arrangement, and he brought her very forward indeed, considering the short time. She did *this* with him, ma'am, and *this*," pointing to Nessy's millboard studies suspended against the wall.

"What, can she paint in oils? Dear me, how very singular!" Then, after a little pause, "Your daughter must be a superior person, Mrs. Saffery; perhaps older than she looks."

"Only fourteen, ma'am."

"Oh, then she looks older than she is!"

After this there was a marked difference in her manner to Nessy, which Nessy felt very gratifying, though she did not guess its origin.

Another Sunday came and went. There were considerable additions to the number of Sunday scholars; and, to Nessy's great joy, Mr. Weir made his appearance among them, though his stay was only to be from Saturday to Monday. His presence seemed to wind them all up; but there were really too many girls for a single class, so a subdivision was made, and a great girl of twelve years old, Susan Potter, was installed its teacher, to her own great elation. She performed her part exceedingly well. All were orderly and obedient, not a single black mark was yet entered in the awful book, consisting of a quire of mourning note-paper, with broad black borders, which, in a black leather cover, was known as the black book. Mr. Weir's teachings increased in spirituality as they proceeded. He began with a short extempore prayer, and then invited the boys to find and read aloud sundry texts relating to prayer and its answer; and, by reiterated efforts, in his earnest, winning way, he got them to see, understand, and feel something of the wonderful compassion of God in being actually more willing to hear than we to pray. After exemplifying it in one way and another, by illustrations suited to their capacities, he looked about on them with a hearty, "Now, is not it wonderful, boys?" And there was genuine sincerity in the sober reply of some of them. "Yes, it's very wonderful, sir."

Afterwards he spoke some encouraging words to Nessy and to Susan Potter, and, as they left the schoolroom, he asked Nessy if she had been confirmed.

"Not yet, sir; I was too young at our last confirmation."

"Well, you will not be too young for the next. Let your preparation for it begin from this hour. Be in a state of preparedness."

"I hardly know what to do, sir."

"The Bible will assist you, if you seek it for information. I do not want to bind you down by slavish rules; but I shall soon settle in my new home, and will give you a little hint and help from time to time."

CHAPTER XVI.

CLASSES.

Mrs. Homer prevailed upon herself to get ready for church in time to walk up the aisle just as Dr. Fownes entered the reading-desk. Poor Dr. Fownes was very feeble now, and his reading was so indistinct, that it was a penalty to hear him; yet he thought himself bound in duty to persist in what many people would have been pleased at his giving up. The singing was of the most primitive kind, led by a flageolet. It was a relief when Mr. Weir's fine voice was heard at the communion-table; and Mrs. Homer, who had furtively been scanning the gayer portion of the congregation with pensive glances, suddenly concentrated her attention. It was very fortunate for her, she thought, that the pew-opener had placed her in a seat immediately opposite the pulpit, so that she would have every advantage in hearing the sermon; and directly it began, she fixed those soft, dark eyes of hers so attentively on Mr. Weir, that, if he had happened to notice her, it might have put him out; but happily his eager looks seemed to seek out his congregation in every direction but hers. He was very full of his subject, which was on the text, "Hearken, ye careless daughters;" and as there were many careless daughters in church, some of them felt the address to be personal, and bridled up, while others humbly took it home, and resolved, for the moment at least, that it should do them good; and others, careless heretofore, were careless now, and never even heard the rebukes addressed to careless womanhood in general, but composedly carried on other trains of thought. There could be no doubt that the congregation had become very slothful; and the young clergyman, in his desire to carry out sweeping reforms, was exerting almost too much force at the first start. Yet he undoubtedly commanded attention; many who were accustomed regularly to 'lay up their feet and think of nothing,' listened to him with earnest and somewhat uneasy inquiry in their faces, while the very tones which enchained their half-unwilling ears acted at length as a soporific on Mrs. Homer, whose white lids gradually closed over her eyes in soft repose. Raising those fringed lashes after a time with a little start, she met Nessy's eyes, as ill-luck would have it, and instantly tried to look innocent. Nessy was perhaps more ashamed of catching her napping than she was of being caught, and for some minutes neither could think of anything else.

Nor would Mrs. Homer's conscience let the matter rest. At dinner, she said to Nessy—

"Mr. Weir is a very powerful preacher,—a very interesting man. I can't think how it was that the latter part of his sermon made me so lethargic. It is a mistake, I think, to make sermons so long. Perhaps I should keep up my attention better if I used tablets. Who were those pretty girls in pink?"

"The Miss Grevilles, ma'am."

"Oh! And who was the lady with the blue and white feather?"

"Mrs. Poyntz, ma'am."

"There was rather an elegant woman in a black lace shawl."

"Lady Clive, ma'am."

" Lady Clive ? Oh, indeed ! What, of Belforest Park ? "

" Yes, ma'am."

And in this way she went idly on, without considering that she was detaining the family from their dinner.

The evenings were drawing in now, and after they were shut in for the night, she sought solace in her harp, and felt her way through Martin Luther's hymn, pausing between each chord—

" While one with moderate haste might count a hundred,"

but never playing a false note, and making the air vibrate with melody.

" Very harmonious," said Mr. Saffery, at the conclusion, after listening intently with his hands on his knees, and his head a little on one side.

" One would like to know a little more about that young lady," observed Mrs. Saffery, and to be sure that all's right."

" All's right ? " repeated her husband ; " why, what should be wrong ? Don't go and take away an innocent young person's good name by hoping that all's right. Many a fair fame has been tarnished by innuendos like that."

"Dear me, Saffery! I really was thinking no harm. You took me up too short."

"Well, I didn't mean to do that; but you should be cautious what you say. Wasn't she recommended to us by Miss Antony? And we know who she corresponds with—Miss Crow, of Ipswich, and Messrs. Root and Branche, Lincoln's Inn. There can't be anything to sound more respectable than that."

"I wonder if Miss Antony really did send her, though," said Mrs. Saffery. "We've only her own word for it."

"Betsy, I'm ashamed of you," said Mr. Saffery, with asperity. "Is this fit for Sunday evening talk? I shall go and stamp the letters."

And soon was heard the clip-clop, clip-clop, clip-clop, with more energy and determination than ever.

"I'm sure I wish I'd bit my tongue before ever I spoke," said Mrs. Saffery. "This comes of having music practising on Sundays, just as if there were not six week-day evenings for tweedle-deeing. Nessy, you've one of your bad headaches, I can see. That comes of the Sunday-schooling."

“ My head does ache a little,” said Nessy ; “ but it was not so bad till you and my papa had words.”

“ Words ? ” repeated Mrs. Saffery. “ I really wonder, sometimes, at the unfounded things people go and say. What words did your father and I have, pray ? He told me to be cautious, and I said I was thinking no harm. Sure, such remarks as those may pass between a husband and wife without their being accused of having words. Don’t you ever go, Nessy, and make mischief between husband and wife, and, least of all, between your father and mother.”

Nessy brushed away a tear.

“ Your head won’t be better till you’ve had a good night’s sleep, depend upon it,” said Mrs. Saffery, in a softer tone. “ I begin to regret that I ever let you go to the Sunday-school.”

“ Oh, mother ! ”

“ Yes, Nessy, because it is very hard work ; and though its increasing so fast shows how much it was needed, the burthen is too heavy on you. Why should *you* be the only unpaid fag ? I’m sure that every word Mr. Weir said

to-day applied to the Miss Grevilles and Miss
Sturt and Miss Badger and Miss Hornblower,
and not a bit of impression did it make—they
were laughing and giggling directly they got
outside the churchyard; and there was somebody, who is not a hundred miles off, that had
a comfortable nap."

Nessy was sorry her mother had seen it, but
could not help smiling. Mrs. Saffery saw the
smile.

"Come," said she, "take your Bible and
read a chapter to me, for my eyes don't bear
much reading now; and after that you may
bring out the cold meat for supper."

Mr. Saffery came in as Nessy was in the
middle of her chapter, and reverently sat down
and listened, with his head inclining a little
towards her. Those good words were very
solemnizing and edifying to them all. And
then they gathered round rather a better
supper than usual, and ate it cheerfully and
thankfully.

"Saffery, here's just such a little brown bit
as you prefer."

"You have it."

"No; I've enough on my plate. Come, you

can find room for this. Nessy, there's the parlour-bell."

Nessy went and returned.

" What is the lady doing?" (in an under-tone.)

" Writing."

Mr. Saffery could not help saying, with a little malice—

" If that had been a proper inquiry, you needn't have dropped your voice."

" There was nothing improper in it."

" Suppose she were to ask what *we* were about."

" She did, last Sunday, and I heard Nessy's answer—' Family prayers.' "

" Nothing to be ashamed of, at any rate."

" No ; I thought it set a good lesson."

" Why, how *can* she have family prayers when she's all by herself?" cried Mr. Saffery. " The unreasonableness of women ! I don't think you've one bit of compassion for your sex. If you were bereaved, or bereft, which-ever is the right word, like that young creature, would you like sitting evening after evening by yourself, all the long evenings, by the light of two mould sixes, without a creature to speak

a word of comfort or to think a kind thought
of you ?"

"No, Saffery, I shouldn't.   I hope that will
never be my case, my good man."

"Pity her whose case it is, then."

"I do, in a way, and I should do so more,
if I knew how much she pitied herself.   Somehow, she seems to have those soft looks and
little sighs at command.   I never see her with
red eyes.   This couldn't be the case (unless
she were a flint), if she had lost such a husband
as you, Saffery."

"Ah! such as me don't grow on every
bush," said he, holding his hand to her and
giving hers a good squeeze.   "We've jogged
on many a year, old lady, and shall, I hope,
jog on a many more.   But howsoever many,
there must come the last of them at last."

The tender fall in his voice, and Mrs.
Saffery's moistened eyes, were very touching
to Nessy.

Next morning, when Mr. Weir brought his
letters to post, he stepped into the shop, and
said—

"Good morning, Miss Saffery.   You had
one of your bad headaches yesterday, I could

sec. It shall not occur again if I can provide against it. You shall have plenty of help next Sunday."

"Oh, sir, I don't want any!" cried Nessy, in alarm. "I'd much rather go on by myself."

"Why, you're like the man in the 'Midsummer Night's Dream,' who wanted to play all the parts himself. How can you carry on four classes? And four classes there will be, besides mine, counting the little tots, who must form a separate class till we get an infant-school."

Nessy looked much disturbed.

"Have you secured any other teachers, then, sir?"

"The Miss Grevilles have sent in their names. Is Mrs. Homer at home?"

Nessy replied that she was.

"Take her this card, then, and say I shall be obliged if she can grant me a few minutes on business. Say that I would not intrude on her so early, but that I return to London by the 12·30 train."

Nessy obeyed; and returned, saying very gravely, that Mrs. Homer would be happy to see him. She showed him in, and saw Mrs. Homer's look of distant politeness as she rose and gravely bowed. Then she closed the door on them, and resumed her needlework, thinking that an important interview was about to take place. Her headache came on again.

Whether the interview were important or not, Mr. Weir appeared not to care about its being public, for he spoke in such an animated tone, that it seemed as if it would have been easy to Nessy to hear every word he said, though that was just what she either could not do or was too honourable to do. Mrs. Homer's soft voice was scarcely audible. Meanwhile, the mid-day post came in, and there was the usual bustle in the shop. Just as the London mail-bag was sent off, and the Safferys were in the midst of their sorting the letters that had arrived, Mr. Weir opened the parlour-door, saying, cheerfully—

" Well, then, I shall depend on you. I shall expect great things. Don't be diffident. It will all come easy, you will see. There is nothing to discourage. You will take great interest in it in a little time. You know where to—" (lowering his voice, and stepping back to say a few earnest words).

" Ah, yes !—yes, indeed ! "

Then they shook hands, and he passed rapidly through the shop, saying to Nessy, with a smile—

" The train is almost due, and I have no time to lose. But I've secured another ally."

And she could but call up a smile in return, though she felt it no smiling matter.

" What did he mean by ally ? " said Mrs. Saffery, when he was gone.

" He meant that he has got Mrs. Homer to try to teach in the Sunday-school," said Nessy, " and the Miss Grevilles are going to take classes."

" Then he has done a good morning's work," said Mrs. Saffery, with strong approval. " Think of his getting the Miss Grevilles to condescend ! Your head will have a better chance now ; and I'm glad in my heart that Mrs. Homer is going to try her hand at something useful."

" But," said Nessy, in a very low voice, " I don't believe she'll do a bit of good ; it is not in her way. I don't think the children will mind her when they find she can't teach them."

" Why can't she teach them?"

Nessy did not like to say; but her mother *would* have an answer.

" She is very sweet and gentle," said Nessy; " but I don't fancy her to care much for little children, or for Scripture teaching."

" Well, time will show," said Mrs. Saffery, who was not at all disposed to quarrel with the arrangement. " It will get her up earlier in the morning for one thing; and if she finds her deficiencies, she'll be less set up."

" As for my head, I believe it will be all the worse instead of the better for it," said Nessy. " There will be such a chatter, it will be all confusion."

" Don't go and meet troubles half-way, Nessy. Here comes Mr. Greville's four-in-hand."

The open carriage, with two or three pretty, lady-like girls in it, drew up for a moment, while the footman descended from his perch to inquire for their letters. Having received them, he delivered them to the ladies, who began reading them as they drove off.

Nessy, going into the parlour to lay the cloth, found Mrs. Homer pensively leaning on her hand near the window.

"That was a stylish turn-out," said she, looking round. "The Grevilles?"

"Yes, ma'am."

"They are elegant girls. Do you know their Christian names?"

"Emily and Sophia."

"How charming! Do they visit any one here?"

"Oh, no, ma'am! They're quite in a class above the village. They call on Mrs. Fownes sometimes."

"Mr. Weir is awakening in them an interest for the poor. He lunched with them yesterday on purpose. And he met Lady Clive and talked to her about mothers' meetings. She did not know about them, and I can't say I do. He got the Miss Grevilles to undertake classes at the Sunday-school. How zealous he is!"

"Very zealous!" said Nessy.

"He has offered me a class, too," said Mrs. Homer, "and as the Miss Grevilles have joined, I don't see why I should not accept it.

I suppose I ought to consider it a compliment. I tried to escape—told him I knew nothing— was quite an ignoramia—at which he only smiled."

"You will find it very interesting, ma'am," said Nessy, "when once you take it up heartily."

"It all depends," said she, languidly. "I don't know that I can take interest in anything of that kind now," she added, rather tardily.

During dinner, she asked Nessy to give her some idea of the routine. Nessy did her best, but did not make much of it; and Mrs. Homer, after a little meditation, observed that she thought it might be much better in the hands of a paid person.

"However," said she, "Mr. Weir has set his mind on it, and what he sets his mind on, we may be sure he will effect. Few could help conceding what he asked, he has such an interesting way with him. Do you think it will rain?"

"No, ma'am, I see no sign of it."

"Then let Roberto bring round the little carriage."

Finding the boy did not and would not answer to the name of Lubin, Mrs. Homer had been obliged to make his own name rather more Arcadian by adding an o final, at first sportively, and now habitually.

While she was out, a good-tempered looking old farmer, who might have sat or stood for the model of Ready-money Jack, called for a money-order, and likewise to ask his friend and gossip, Mr. Saffery, whether he had not a lodger named Homer.

" That I have," said Mr. Saffery. " D'ye know anything about her ? "

" No," said Farmer Benson ; " that's the very question I meant to put to you."

At which they both laughed.

" Oh ! she's a nicish sort of lady," said Mr. Saffery. " Not at home this afternoon."

" No ; I saw her go down street. Safe, I suppose ? You had references ? "

" Well, we didn't even ask for any," said Mr. Saffery, " because she came recommended— at least, she said she came recommended—by a prior lodger of ours—at least, the lodger's sister."

" That doesn't sound like much of a voucher," said the farmer, doubtfully.

"But she's as safe as the Bank, I believe."

"Which bank ?" said Farmer Benson, quickly, for a country bank had lately broken, whereby he had sustained some loss.

They laughed again ; and Mr. Saffery said, "The Bank of England was what I was thinking of. She pays regular, by the week ; has done so ever since my good wife hinted to her the rule of former lodgers. She said, quite pleasantly, ' Oh ! such is the custom of Branksome Hall, is it ? It makes no difference to me. Never mind.' "

"Well, she has a pleasant way with her, that's a fact," said the farmer ; "and bewidowed so young and all ! I should think all was safe enough, only I thought I'd just inquire quietly; for, you see, she's thinking of taking land."

"Oh ! is she ?" said Mr. Saffery, with interest.

"Has been to me twice," said the farmer, "about a piece I can't nohow make over to her, because I get my very best wheat off it. I've told her she may have the pick of Brushworth and Stubblecroft, but she off-and-ons about them, because she says they're not picturskew."

"Does she want many acres?" said Mr. Saffery.

"Well, I can hardly make out what she does want," said Farmer Benson, "because she changes her mind so.   Is that her natur'?"

"Why, I can scarcely tell," said Mr. Saffery; "for she has nothing to change her mind about here except her dinner, and she mostly begins by ordering what we can't in possibility get for her, and ends by putting up with whatever we have."

"Obliging, at any rate," said the farmer.

"Quite so. Oh! I think you needn't be afraid of her."

"Here comes our little painter," said Farmer Benson, holding out his broad hand to Nessy. He had bought the largest of her pictures.

"You had better come some afternoon," said he, "and see how well it looks over the mantel-piece."

CHAPTER XVII.

THE OLD LADY.

Nessy's forebodings were but too closely verified on Sunday morning. Punctually as she
kept her appointment, there was a little cluster,
not only of teachers, but of supernumeraries, in
the middle of the schoolroom, talking very fast
and all together, with their faces almost touching each other's bonnets. Around them, but
at a respectful distance, stood knots of silent
children, who seemed much surprised and dis-
comfited at the presence of strangers. Nessy
immediately formed a nucleus for these little
stragglers, who, at a signal from her, instantly
drew about her in a well-ordered semicircle,
pressing closer to her than usual, that they
might hear her gentle voice amid the confusion
of tongues. The ladies stared at her, and then
exchanged expressive looks and shrugs, as much
as to say, " Is *this* the way our allotted charges

are to be taken from us ? We *knew* it would be no use coming ! " Then a party of boys, in thick boots, clattered in with much noise and little respect for fine ladies. Then Mrs. Homer darkened the doorway, looking curiously about her, and seeming in suspense whether to advance or retreat; then bestowing an arch look at Nessy, who greeted her with a smile of welcome, and quietly crossing the room to her. Every look, every step of her progress was noticed by the ladies, who silently scrutinized her from top to toe with open impertinence, and then huddled yet closer together to exchange remarks. Nessy had not supposed real ladies could be so ill-bred, and thought how much Mrs. Homer gained by comparison with them. She spoke to her in a low tone, and told her what there was to do, and how to do it ; and while thus engaged, they started at Mr. Weir's clear, authoritative, somewhat aggrieved utterance of—

"Come, teachers ! "

Dead silence. Then he gravely took his place and said,—

" Let us pray."

Down knelt boys and girls, Nessy and Mrs.

Homer; there was a prodigious rustling of silks, taken up that they might by no means come in contact with the floor, among the select specimens of the upper ten thousand, some of whom knelt in very uncomfortable and unusual attitudes. Mr. Weir prayed that a spirit of order, and unanimity, and humility, and heavenly-mindedness might prevail among them all, and that the blessed Spirit might not disdain to visit such lowly temples as their hearts, but might so fill them with its sweet and purifying influences, that there should be no room for any evil or trifling spirit to enter. One might have thought such a prayer might have sunk into all his intelligent assistants' hearts; and the Miss Grevilles did rise sobered; but their bevy of companions clustered round Mr. Weir directly they were off their knees, and tittered as one of them said—

"Oh, Mr. Weir, we're supernumeraries, please; we are not going to interfere with your work. We only came to keep the Miss Grevilles in countenance, and start them off."

He bent his head a little and said—

" We have no room for supernumeraries here, nor any need or time for those who do not work."

Rather abashed, they fluttered out of the
school, whispering and giggling directly they
crossed its threshold. The Miss Grevilles
looked rather ashamed, and listened attentively
to Mr. Weir's brief directions, which they
immediately did their best to fulfil. He
turned with a pleased look to Nessy and
Mrs. Homer, each with her orderly little class
before her, and said—

" *You* need no monition, either of you. I
may look for unqualified, genuine help from
you."

Mrs. Homer repaid him by her sweetest
smile, and Nessy felt very happy. Now that
the supernumeraries were dismissed, everything
fell into order; there was a continuous hum,
but it was easy to hear one's self speak, which,
just before, had really not been the case.

" I am going to say a few words," began Mr.
Weir. You might have heard a pin drop.
He addressed them for a few minutes, explain-
ing anew to them all why they were there,
what they must keep in view, and in what
spirit they must try to attain it. Then they
all recommenced with fresh spirit, and Nessy
began to be glad some of the burthen was

taken from her. She glanced now and then at Mrs. Homer, to see how she prospered, and observed her occasionally at fault. The children had read their little portion, and she did not seem to have many questions to ask. Once or twice they came to a dead stop. Then, after much consideration, she asked the little girl nearest to her—

"Who was Paul?"

No answer. "Can't you tell me who Paul was?" Not one of them could or would tell.

"He was an apostle—a very good man."

She yawned a little behind her glove. One after another all the children yawned. Nessy was in pain for her, and glad when Mr. Weir gave out the concluding hymn.

The Miss Grevilles were shy of singing in a Sunday-school. Nessy was shy of singing close to the Miss Grevilles. Mrs. Homer's self-possession stood her in good stead. She followed the lead very nicely, and then Nessy took courage, and then the Miss Grevilles took courage; and the blended voices sounded very sweetly. Then, after the benediction, the Miss Grevilles glanced at Mrs. Homer and Nessy, and stood irresolute for a moment, but decided *not* to fraternize with them, and, with a little bow to Mr. Weir, flitted away. He looked after them, rather disappointed, and said to Mrs. Homer—

"I meant you to have made friends together, but another time will do."

"Oh, don't give it a thought; it doesn't in the least signify," said she, with her charming smile.

At Mrs. Homer's dinner, Nessy could not resist saying—

"I was so glad, ma'am, you led the singing so courageously! We were all very cowardly."

"Oh," said Mrs. Homer, "it did not require much confidence to sing to such an audience as *that*. I have had my courage more severely tried! And I did not think it worth while to throw my voice out—I just hummed a little, for the sake of the children."

"I knew," said Nessy, "that I was not singing to the Miss Grevilles, but—to the Lord; therefore it was wrong to feel ashamed, and I conquered it as soon as I could."

"Ah," said Mrs. Homer, carelessly, "I regret to say I did not take so high a view of the matter as you did."

"Are you not glad, ma'am, you went?"

"Well—yes—no—there was not much satisfaction in it. I knew I was pleasing Mr. Weir, so that supported me; but he did not know of the insulting contempt of those supernumeraries. I was glad to see them walk off."

"So was I, very glad indeed," said Nessy. "I wonder at their assurance in coming."

"Oh, there was nothing in it; and nothing to keep them out. I don't desire to meet them again. I should like to know the Miss Grevilles, I own."

"They had a great mind to speak, I think," said Nessy.

"And a greater mind not to speak. But I'm used to the ways of this curious world. I don't mind it; it does not in the least signify."

To refresh herself after her morning's toils, she took a long nap in the afternoon; and as the Miss Grevilles had already told Mr. Weir their mamma would not allow them to come to the school a second time in the day, Nessy rejoiced in having the afternoon classes entirely under the conduct of herself and Susan Potter, who had not been able to attend in the morning.

These two girls, one under fifteen, the other

turned twelve, had such zeal, sense, and goodness, that Mr. Weir might well entrust to them the chief weight of the school. For it is not always age that is needful to make a good teacher or a good nurse.

Nessy made friends with Susan Potter, the baker's daughter, for, thought she, though my mamma says my education places me above her, the Miss Grevilles are clearly much farther above me; and how pleased I should have been if they had given me, or even had only given Mrs. Homer, a kind word!

The following Sunday, the Miss Grevilles seemed rather ashamed of their exclusiveness, and made some advances. They came up to Nessy, whom they knew well by sight, and the eldest said rather gravely, but kindly—

"You are very constant at your work, Miss Saffery. You undertake more than we can do, in coming twice a day."

"I like coming," said Nessy, simply.

And after the classes were dismissed, the elder sister, closely followed by the younger, spoke to Mrs. Homer, and said—

"There has been good attendance to-day. How much the school was wanted!"

Mrs. Homer looked upwards and smiled; as much as to say—

"Oh, *so* wanted !"

Miss Emily Greville then took courage to say—

"It was rather embarrassing at first; but I get on better now, and like it."

"*So* embarrassing at first," said Mrs. Homer.

This was all that passed; and if there had been more, it would only have increased subsequent mortification; for Mrs. Greville, finding that her daughters had been guilty of these small amenities to a stranger and a nobody, told them "it would not do;" they must beware of entangling themselves in acquaintanceships they could not keep up: she had very reluctantly acceded to Mr. Weir's wish that they should take classes, and they must either keep their co-helpers at a proper distance, or give up their attendance.

So, the following Sunday, the Miss Grevilles made the stiffest, slightest inclination of the head when Mrs. Homer and Nessy came in, and abruptly engaged themselves with their pupils, to prevent the possibility of exchanging a word; feeling very uncomfortable, poor girls

in this strict obedience to orders, for they were
young and thin-skinned. They left the schoolroom almost precipitately as soon as the classes
broke up, to the keen mortification of Mrs.
Homer, who had intended the opening already
made to be improved. She said at dinner to
Nessy—

"Those Miss Grevilles are inconsistent girls,
I think; one never knows where to have them.
Last Sunday they spoke civilly; to-day they
would scarcely bow. It makes the attendance
very unpleasant, when one is subjected to such
slights. However, I don't mind it, that's one
comfort!"

Nessy had put Mrs. Homer more *au courant*
with respect to the routine, so that she now
got through her duty not discreditably; but as
her heart was not really in it, it was rather
unimproving and irksome to her scholars and
herself. Sometimes, on returning from a walk,
she would say, "I returned by way of Fairlee
Common, and stood looking at your cottage,
Miss Saffery. 'Tis a pretty, *pretty* place : I
only wish it were mine. I have seen nothing
that has taken my fancy so much ; and building
seems to be very expensive. Besides, what a

long time a house takes building. Sometimes I think of taking a common labourer's cottage, and just adding to it; it is a very anxious matter to frame one's self a home."

"I wonder, ma'am," Mrs. Saffery would say, "that an elegant lady like you should think of burying yourself in a place like this."

Then said Mrs. Homer, "When the heart is buried, Mrs. Saffery, one may as well be buried altogether."

Meanwhile, Mr. Weir and his mother took possession of the cottage. He had told Mrs. Homer that he should bring his mother to call on her, which was like cutting a Gordian knot, because it seemed a difficult point to Mrs. Homer which of them should call first, if there were to be any calling—she not being a resident, but yet the first comer. She was very glad to have the matter settled by him, for she certainly wanted to be on friendly terms with mother and son. But she had said, "I cannot expect Mrs. Weir to call on a mere lodger, though I hope to have a pretty place of my own by-and-by. I quite long to have a place to lay my weary head!"

"My mother and I do not estimate people

by their houses," said Mr. Weir. "We are going into a small one ourselves."

"Oh, *your* cottage is perfection. I envy you it."

"Ah, I know you were disappointed of it; but I could not give it up—there was no other place for me. You may soon run yourself up a pretty, ornamental cottage—prettier, in fact, than mine."

She shook her head, and smiled.

Mrs. Saffery went to the cottage to put the new comers in possession, and returned very full of what she had seen. "Mrs. Weir is a stout old lady," said she, "short and red-faced. I never knew a shorter mother of a tall son. She's a sharp one, you may depend on it. She scanned the place in a moment, peeped into every hole and corner, tasted the water, held the tumbler up to the light, inquired about the drainage, the poor-rate and highway-rate—how many butchers there were, and which was the best—what was the price of bread and coals— what firewood we chiefly used—what soil the cottage was built on—where was the nearest fire-engine—who was the constable—and ever so many other things. She's a manager, and so you'll find."

"To be of any use, she should have made her inquiries before the cottage was taken," said Mr. Saffery.

"She couldn't, for he took it before he told her; and you know, Saffery, it was a good thing he took it so quick, for if he hadn't, Mrs. Homer would have had it."

Mrs. Homer awaited her visitors rather anxiously, for, if Mrs. Weir called on her, others might call, and she began to feel her solitude rather monotonous, without

> "Some friend in her retreat,
> To whom to whisper, 'Solitude is sweet.'"

At length, after much vacillating, she thought Mrs. Weir might be waiting for her to take the first step, and determined to leave a card. She left a card, and told the neat maid-servant she hoped Mrs. Weir was recovering from her fatigue; for Mrs. Weir had brought her own maid-servant, not much approving of her son's description of Mrs. Early, who remained in the house, but out of sight.

The same afternoon, Mr. Weir, coming into the post-office for stamps, met Mrs. Homer, and said—

"My mother is much obliged to you for your kind inquiries. She will return calls by-and-by, but at present is hardly settled."

"Oh! I can quite understand that," said Mrs. Homer. "I can quite feel for her."

"Oh! she is not exactly a subject for compassion," returned he, laughing. "In fact, she is quite in her element. She is very fond of domestic occupation, and will be a great help to me in the parish some day."

As he quitted the shop, Mrs. Homer murmured, half to herself, and half to Nessy, whom she felt to be a sympathizer—

"'Julia's a manager, she's born to rule;'"

a line which Nessy never afterwards forgot. And she knew quite well who was meant, and could never help smiling when Mrs. Homer now and then said, quietly—

"Here comes Julia."

Well, the visit was returned at last, but not without a stout remonstrance on Mrs. Weir's part. She said—

"Frank, how could you commit me so, by telling Mrs. Homer I should call upon her?"

"I thought you *would* call upon her," re-

plied he. " I thought you would call on everybody."

" But she is only a lodger, a summer-visitor ;
she is not known to anybody here."

" My dear mother, she is at any rate a fellow-
creature ; and my affair, and I hope yours, is
to do good to as many fellow-creatures as we
can reach, without considering whether they
live in lodgings or houses of their own."

This was the way Mrs. Weir declared
Frank always shut her up. She was very
fond of telling those whom she admitted to
the privileges of intimacy, that she had been
a complete worldling till Frank converted her.
And the corollary she very plainly deduced
from it, was—" And since he has converted
me, why shouldn't you let him convert *you* ? "

" What makes you like her so ? " she said,
as they started together for the visit, " She's
very pretty, I suppose."

" She is very interesting and sweet-tempered.
No one without a sweet temper could have
taken the Miss Balfours' contumely as she
did ; even her position, as a young widow, calls
for sympathy, and she wishes to be useful."

"Young widows are very ensnaring."

VOL. I.   S

"One would think *you* were not a widow," said he, cheerfully. "How can you be so hard on a younger sister?"

The old lady gave him one of her droll looks, which told him he had not made a bit of impression; so they talked of other things.

Happily Mrs. Homer was at home, with everything pretty about her, as far as the little room could be made pretty; and she welcomed her visitors with the sweetest smiles.

"You have got over your fatigues, I hope," said she, almost tenderly.

"Oh, nothing fatigues me," said Mrs. Weir, "except having nothing to do; and that will never be the case here, I can easily see. I never saw a place more run to waste: *you've* taken up the schools, I hear; how do you get on?"

And Mrs. Homer had, from this point, to stand a close cross-examination, not only on school-rooms, school-teachers, school-children, and school-books, but a variety of subjects which she was unprepared to be catechized on. Mrs. Weir did not exactly ask her how long she had been widowed, what her husband had been, and what he had died of; but she approached it as nearly as she possibly could. She did ask her if she had ever had the conduct of a town or country parish; whether she had lived mostly in one neighbourhood or had gone about much; whether she had determined to settle here for a permanence; whether she had anything in view yet; whether she knew Mrs. Fownes, or the Grevilles, &c. &c.

Mr. Weir endeavoured to soften his mother's bluntness as much as he could, and Mrs. Homer took refuge in soft looks and monosyllables, and tried to carry the war into the enemy's country by asking questions in return: whether Mrs. Weir found the house perfectly dry, whether the garden was in good order, whether there would be a good winter crop of potatoes, &c. &c. When they were gone, and Nessy came in to lay the cloth, she relieved herself by drawing a deep breath, and saying,

"What a terrific old lady!"

CHAPTER XVIII.

FRIENDSHIP CEMENTED.

SHALL I be believed if I say that two days from this visit, the terrific old lady and Mrs. Homer were on the best of terms? The way it came to pass was this :—

A fine, mellow, autumnal afternoon had tempted Mrs. Homer to walk to Daisylands, and work once more on Farmer Benson's feelings about the piece of ground he had no mind to sell. The farmer was not expected home before night, for he had gone to an annual " beast market ; " so Mrs. Homer had only her walk for her pains,—at least it seemed so, but events often turn out different from what they seem.

She turned away a little disappointed, for the old farmer's honest blue eyes told her plainly he thought her worth looking at, and he always spoke to her cheerily. The white farmhouse, backed by magnificent elms, stood surrounded by almost a little town of outhouses, stables, granaries, and sheds, with enormous ricks in the back-ground. Mrs. Homer had daintily picked her way through the slushy yards to see the cows and the horses, and the pigs, and the dairy; and had followed the farmer up the neat gravel-walk of his garden to see the bee-hives, and admire his fruit-trees; so that she knew the premises well, and sometimes she had thought she should like to lodge here rather than at the post-office; but Mrs. Benson did not seem inclined to accede to it.

Passing through the little white gate and along the country by-road, she came to a stile which led to what was called "the hilly field." Now, this hilly field adjoined Fairlee Common, and was, in fact, a piece taken off it. It was a short cut to the village, and a very pretty walk besides, boasting particularly fine grass, and picturesquely bordered with hedgerow timber.

Nobody being in sight, Mrs. Homer cleared the stile in a way that none but the young and very agile can do. She sprang over it, scarcely touching the third bar with her right foot, and the top bar with her left, and was on the other side the next moment. Having accomplished this feat, she took a little foot-track to the left, amused at herself for what she had done, not having, in fact, done anything so childish for some years, and being carried back by it to memories of younger times.

Having ascended the little slope which gave the field its name, she saw, hastening up its opposite side, Mrs. Weir, at a pace very inconvenient to a woman of her age and size; and secretly rejoiced that her clearing the stile had not been seen by that lady. Mrs. Weir's face, always inclining to red, was now rubicund with heat and fear: and when Mrs. Homer civilly accosted her with "Good morning, ma'am," she said, in a troubled voice,—

"My dear, there's a mad bull!"

Mrs. Homer changed colour, and looked hastily round. There was a herd feeding on the lower ground, and nearer at hand a pond.

"Are you sure the animal is mad?" said she. "Perhaps he is only going to drink."

"Hear the low mumbling he is making; I'm sure he's not all right."

"Suppose we keep round this side of the pond."

"We shall be farther from the gate."

"Yes, but he cannot be on both sides of the pond at once."

"Now, he has his eye on us," cried Mrs. Weir, excitedly—"now he is coming towards us! he'll cut us off! Oh, my dear! run, run while you can—I can't, for I'm too heavy."

"No, I won't forsake you," said Mrs. Homer, who was very pale. "Give me your hand— don't be frightened — let us look at him steadily."

Gradually approaching the pond, and likewise approaching their enemy, they reached its brink at last, and so did he; and then, to their immense relief, he began to drink. Oh, what a deep-drawn breath Mrs. Weir gave, and how heartily she thanked Mrs. Homer, who begged her not to think of it!

"I can't think enough of it," replied she. "You showed real self-possession, and real unselfishness, too, for our danger was in common, and what hindered your running away except your thoughtfulness for me? I shall not forget it, I assure you."

And all across the common she talked garrulously to the gratified Mrs. Homer, who accompanied her to her own gate; and then she insisted on her going in, and pressed her to stay to tea.

"No cap? Oh, never mind being in your hair for once. Or I'll lend you one; or you can keep on your bonnet; or Mary shall run down for your own."

This last offer was accepted, so Mary was sent off with a message to Nessy; and meanwhile Mrs. Weir took her visitor over the cottage, and pointed out its merits and deficiencies, took credit to herself for various contrivances, and asked her opinion of others in contemplation.

When Mr. Weir came in and found Mrs. Homer winding knitting-cotton for his mother, he looked surprised enough, but very much pleased; and was more pleased when Mrs. Weir told him graphically how Mrs. Homer had been her preserver. It gave rise to a good deal of laughing, too, for he could not be persuaded that there had been any real danger; "But if you thought there was," said he, "it amounted to the same thing. Did *you* feel really frightened, Mrs. Homer?"

"I should not have thought of being so," she

replied, "if it had not been for Mrs. Weir's alarm, but fear is contagious."

"Ah, my mother, for a strong-minded woman, has some singular fears; of every little yap-yapping dog, for instance."

"Yes, I have a great objection to being bitten," said Mrs. Weir, "and special fears of hydrophobia."

"But barking dogs don't bite."

"Oh, don't they, though! I know to the contrary."

"Yes, so do I," said Mrs. Homer.

"You partake of my mother's fears, then."

"I like large, generous dogs, with amiable eyes.   And they always like me."

"They see that you like them, and love your caressing them.   Ah, we generally like those who like and caress us!"

"Oh, yes, it is instinctive."

"Do you see much of Miss Saffery, Mrs. Homer?"

"In a sort of a way, of course.   She waits on me.   I don't make her a companion, of course."

"*Is* that of course?   The poor girl has aspirations and capacities above her position."

"Is it good for girls to have aspirations

above their position ?" interposed Mrs. Weir. "*I* think not."

"It depends, mother, on the nature of the aspirations. Miss Saffery does not aspire to dress like the Miss Grevilles, or to be noticed by them."

"I should hope not, indeed!"

"But for one so young, and with so few intellectual advantages, she has a cultivated mind."

"Does her cultivated mind permit her to mend her father's stockings?" said Mrs. Weir.

"Yes, it really does," said Mrs. Homer. "She is a very good, submissive, domestic girl. They are a well-conducted family."

"How do you define a well-conducted family, Mrs. Homer?" said Mr. Weir.

"They have family prayers."

"Family prayers? I should hope so!" said Mrs. Weir.

"Oh, mother, the custom is not too common. It is the exception, rather than the rule, I fear, in that class. You show discrimination, Mrs. Homer, in your example of a well-conducted family. But with regard to making more of a companion of Miss Saffery?"

"Is it not growing late?" said Mrs. Homer. "I fear I must go."

"No; quite early. And I will see you home."

She shook her head and smiled, "*Quite* out of the question."

"And as for Mrs. Homer's making Miss Saffery her companion, Frank, my dear, it's not to be expected; it wouldn't be right," said Mrs. Weir.

"Well, with two against one, I see I've no chance; but what I meant would have broken down no social barriers. A few kind words now and then, a useful hint or encouraging remark."

"Oh, she gets those already, I assure you," said Mrs. Homer.

"That's right; that's what I wanted. I was sure you would."

"Then why could not you let it alone, Frank?" said his mother. "You are but young, yet. Fancy," said she, appealing to Mrs. Homer, "fancy his saddling me with a hobbling old woman who cannot do a thing!"

"Ah, yes!—yes, indeed!" said Mrs. Homer.

"And with an obstinate old man, quite past work!"

" Ah, indeed ! "

" If my mother is going to open on the subject of my delinquencies, I shall be off," said Mr. Weir, laughing.

" I really must go," said Mrs. Homer.

" Mrs. Homer, *do* you know of any one in want of such an old woman as Mrs. Early ? We are really only keeping her out of charity."

" A useless old woman ? "

" I cannot make my mother see," said Mr. Weir, laughing, " that it is better to give the old and infirm a day's wages for a day's work, however poor that work may be, than to pay poor-rates for them to do nothing."

" But, my dear, one's work must be done, and we can only afford one pair of hands ; and if you had looked into the saucepans when we came in, or into the boiler, or at the tin covers, or into the dusthole—"

Mr. Weir and Mrs. Homer joined in a hearty laugh at the idea.

" Ah, you may laugh ; but it is what I had to do, and a good deal besides. My son may pretend to be very philanthropic, Mrs. Homer, but he likes his dinner well cooked, like any other man."

"Oh, mother! I *really* don't care what I have."

"Like any other man," persisted Mrs. Weir; "and if it is to be cooked either by Mrs. Early or me, I know it must be by myself."

"Ah, well, I did not know the case was so hopeless when I engaged her," said Mr. Weir, "but we must give her a little time to look about, at all events. She *must* have a roof over her head."

"That Frenchman, whose name I forget, would have said he didn't see the necessity. And then old Watto. You'll have him muddling about the garden all the winter."

"And a very nice landscape figure he makes, with his thin silver locks stirring in the wind."

"He'll draw on your silver shillings, though, Frank, which are not much thicker than his locks."

"So be it. Of my little, a little I'll give."

"Well, I really *must* go," said Mrs. Homer plaintively.

"Do, my dear, or it will be getting dark; and you have refused Frank's escort. Quite right, quite right. You'll excuse an old woman for speaking her mind. Those are the only

terms on which an old woman can be friends
with a young woman."

"*May* I come again?" said Mrs. Homer,
winningly.

"Of course, of course. Good night, good
night! Frank will see you to the gate."

And Frank accompanied her, without his
hat, several yards beyond the gate. He told
her he was so glad she had made friends with
his mother; he hoped she would drop in very
often. His mother was too old to like making
calls, or to care for company, but she liked
young people—when she *did* like them—and
he could see she liked Mrs. Homer.

Mrs. Homer, on her part, assured him she had
had a most delightful evening. She had taken
to Mrs. Weir from the first; there was something so motherly about her, so genuine! She
only hoped they might be friends—real friends;
there should be no backwardness on *her* part.
She was naturally very fond of old people—old
ladies, especially—and Mrs. Weir was such a
model old lady! But he really must not come
one step farther without his hat. Quite out
of the question. She would not, could not
permit it. She should be home directly, if

hers could be called home. Good night. *Good night.*

"So, Frank, you went farther than the gate?"

"My dear mother, when I came in and found you and Mrs. Homer fraternizing, I *was* surprised!"

"Ah! laugh and welcome. It was no laughing matter to be nearly tossed by a mad bull. She showed great self-possession and kindness in sticking by me as she did, for she *was* frightened, whatever she may say of it—her nice colour died completely away. And there was I 'my dearing' her, and taking tight hold of her hand. Could I cast her off, Frank, directly I reached my own gate?"

"Most certainly not, mother. You did quite right, as you generally do."

"No flattery, sirrah."

"You both did just the thing you ought. You may be comforts to one another, if you will. You are fond of young persons, and like some one to drop in sometimes for a little friendly gossip. Mrs. Homer feels the want of a home and of a motherly friend."

"Did she tell you that, Mr. Frank, between this and the gate?"

"Ah!" said he, mischievously, "a great deal passed between this and the gate. There was so much time for it, and so much inclination!"

Mr. Saffery was putting up his shop-shutters when Mrs. Homer returned. Nessy was lighting the lamp, and directly she saw Mrs. Homer's bright face, she knew she had had a happy evening, and rejoiced at it. How could it be otherwise than delightful to drink tea with Mr. Weir?

Mrs. Homer threw herself on the couch of no repose. She wanted some one to talk to, though it were only Nessy Saffery. She began with—

"I dare say you were surprised enough at my not returning to tea. I had quite an adventure. There was a mad bull in a field— at least, I don't believe the poor creature was mad, but Mrs. Weir was frightened, and I rescued her—not that it was much of a rescue, but I kept by her, instead of running away, and she was so grateful and so pleased, I never saw a woman warm up so. She would make me go in and stay to tea—would take no excuse—offered me one of her own caps, which of course, I would not wear, and then offered to send for mine."

"I am so very glad," said Nessy. "I dare say you had delightful conversation."

"Yes, we had—at least, the old lady said some foolish things, but they drew out Mr. Weir's clever things, and we had a good deal of laughing and chatting. Altogether, we had a very pleasant evening; but I *would* come away early."

"It seems like a reward for your having rescued Mrs. Weir," said Nessy.

"It had not occurred to me in that light, but now you suggest it, it really does seem so. What a very superior young man Mr. Weir is! There's something so excessively interesting about him!"

"Did he see you home, ma'am?"

"No; he offered to do so, but I would not let him. I was obliged to be quite peremptory. He walked with me to the very verge of the common without his hat."

"I hope he won't have the toothache," said Nessy.

"What! with his fine teeth? Besides, the air was balm."

"Would you like a little cold beef for sup-per, ma'am?"

"Well—yes, I think I should."

"I dare say," observed Nessy, as she spread the cloth, "you had a nice talk about the classes."

"On the contrary, they were never once mentioned."

"There," thought Mrs. Homer, as Nessy withdrew, "I have fulfilled Mr. Weir's wishes respecting Miss Saffery. If she does not pre-sume, I will do so again from time to time."

Next day she did not fail to call and inquire how Mrs. Weir felt herself after her fright, and to hope she had experienced no reaction. And she took her Affghan blanket with her to show her what nice candlelight-work it was—only simple knitting—coarse knitting, with one pair of ivory needles, and the arrangement of the colours so excellent! Everything depended on the arrangement of the colours. She would write out the directions if Mrs. Weir liked, and get the wools and pins, and cast on the first row. Then there could be *no* trouble, and it would be such a warm, pleasant wrap for her feet on the sofa, when frost and snow set in.

Mrs. Weir was one of those ladies much given to complain that their eyes will not enable them to do anything useful by candle-light, and yet very averse from bestowing a little time and pains on learning a new employment that promises to be a great resource to them when it ceases to be new. She made a good many objections and excuses, and at last reluctantly yielded consent, and then they got into chat about other things; and as Mrs. Homer had not the privilege of knowing Dr. and Mrs. Fownes, Mrs. Weir had the gratification of telling her how shaky the doctor was, how little fit for duty, how probable it was he would soon be obliged to relinquish it altogether, how he disturbed Mrs. Fownes's rest every night, and what a martyr she was. All this to hear did Mrs. Homer seriously incline, or patiently incline, at any rate; and thenceforth the Affghan blanket became an excuse for almost daily calls on Mrs. Weir, till no excuse was any longer wanting. Sometimes she had a glimpse of Mr. Weir, oftener not; but now and then they had delightful snatches of dialogue, and she was beginning to find quite a new charm in her daily life.

CHAPTER XIX.

MRS. EARLY'S SHORTCOMINGS.

MRS. WEIR was now no longer a terrific old
lady, but a dear, nice old lady, and sometimes a
rather tiresome old lady—when Mr. Weir did
not make his appearance ; but even when Mrs.
Homer thus termed her in her secret heart,
she knew all the while that Mrs. Weir was not
really less nice than usual, but simply that her
appreciation of her niceness had been lessened
by the absence of some one far nicer.

"I really *must* get rid of Mrs. Early," said
Mrs. Weir to her one day. "What do you
think? her attic is just like an old marine-
store shop. I never climbed up to it till this
morning, because the steep stairs try my
breath ; and when I mounted up there, I held
up both my hands ! for there—will you believe
it?—she has stowed all her own wretched
old furniture, till there's hardly room to turn

round ; and when I said *that* musn't be, she began to whimper, and say she had no place to put her things. I am sorry for her, but really cannot have my garret made her Pantechnicon!"

Meanwhile, Mrs. Early was telling her woes across Mr. Saffery's counter to Nessy, and dolefully saying what a hard lady Mrs. Weir was to live with. She had given nothing but satisfaction to Mr. Weir ; he was always contented, and never complained,—never so much as rang the bell oftener than he could help ; but as for Mrs. Weir, she seemed to think a poor person had no feelings, no legs, and yet expected her always to be on them. As to enjoying a refreshing cup of tea, she never allowed such a thing—her word was "quick at work, quick at meat." And she had no consideration for a person not accustomed to go out to service, and thought nothing of her being reduced. She said a servant's wages covered a servant's work; and them that didn't ought to work, didn't ought to eat ! And just as Mrs. Early had come to the conclusion that she must go, Mrs. Weir had told her that go she must; and where in the world should she put her things— her *dirty* old things, Mrs. Weir had unkindly

called them !   But though old, they were not
dirty ; they were as clean as Mrs. Weir's—they
were relics of better days.

Nessy soothed her, and suggested her returning to her old quarters in Providence
Cottages ; but they were engaged. " And if she
turns my things out, there they must stay in
front of the house," whimpered Mrs. Early ;
"and she won't like that—especially the old
coal-scuttle ! "

Nessy observed that no lady could be expected to like it, nor to give warehouse-room to
a servant's household effects.   But what harm
had they done ? retorted Mrs. Early, up in the
garret, which Mrs. Weir had never set foot in
till that morning, and would very likely never
enter again ?   If her son George only knew the
slights put upon his old mother! But George's
bones, too likely, were bleaching in the desert
—she had dreamed they were so, and dreams
were often sent with a purpose. He was his
widowed mother's only son, and so was Mr.
Weir ; and Mrs. Weir ought to take it into
consideration.

Nessy thought so too ; and, by a few kind
words, sent her away consoled ; and then in

came Mrs. Homer, taking the other view of the question, and saying, with a smile, "That was the widow Early, was it not? What a forlorn looking old creature she is! Mrs. Weir says she is quite a discredit to the house, and she thinks her furniture has introduced blackbeetles."

About this time, Mrs. Saffery received a surprise. Mrs. Homer was settling her weekly account, in her usual leisurely, lady-like way, and Mrs. Saffery remarked that she was as punctual and easy to please as Mr. Antony; and then asked Mrs. Homer whether she did not consider him a very nice gentleman?

Mrs. Homer quietly remarked that she had never seen him.

Mrs. Saffery let fall her account in her surprise. "Never seen him?" ejaculated she. "Why, ma'am, Saffery and I considered him your reference."

"How could you do so?" said Mrs. Homer, calmly. "If you had told me you required a reference, I should have referred you to Messrs. Root and Branche; and I will do so now, if you like."

"No, ma'am, no; there's not the least occasion. We know you now, almost as well as Mr. Antony, and you pay so regular, and are so much the lady, that it would be insult to talk of wanting a reference; only when you first came, being a perfect stranger--"

"You thought I might rob the mail-bags," said Mrs. Homer, laughing quietly.

"No, ma'am," and Mrs. Saffery laughed a little too; "only I thought you did say you were recommended to us by Miss Antony."

"So I did, and such was the fact. I met her at the house of a mutual friend during a morning call. I have never seen her brother, though I have seen his pictures at the exhibitions."

Mrs. Saffery uttered a rather dolorous "Oh!"

"Miss Antony and I," continued Mrs. Homer, "were schoolfellows."

"Oh," cried Mrs. Saffery, immensely relieved; "that amounts to the same thing!"

"What does it amount to? We have seldom met since we were schoolgirls."

"No, ma'am; but being at school with Miss Antony seems quite a voucher, for she is such a very nice lady that, somehow, it seems as if every one connected with her must be all right."

"Have you known Miss Antony long?"

"No, ma'am; I have only seen her twice."

"Twice?" repeated Mrs. Homer, "why, you know a great deal more of me, then, than you do of her."

"Well, ma'am," said Mrs. Saffery, twisting the account between her fingers and then smoothing it out; "I know almost nothing of you, but that you are a very nice lady."

"And there is almost nothing to know," said Mrs. Homer, opening her writing-case and taking up her pen, which Mrs. Saffery received as a hint to withdraw.

Talk of a person and he appears. Most of us have verified that proverb occasionally. A day or two after the above dialogue, Nessy was surprised and delighted to see Miss Antony enter the post-office.

"Oh, Miss Antony!" exclaimed she, hastily putting out her hand, and then withdrawing it. Edith saw the movement, and instantly shook hands with her.

"Mrs. Homer is out," said Nessy. "I dare say you have come down to see her."

"No, I did not know she was here," said Edith: "is she in your lodgings, then?"

"Yes, ma'am, she has been here ever since."

"I thought she wanted the cottage?"

"The cottage had just been taken by our new curate, Mr. Weir."

"Oh," said Edith, reflecting a little; and at the same time, Mrs. Saffery came in, delighted to see her, and expressed her hope that Mr. Antony was well.

"He is very far from well," said Edith; "and it is on his account that I have come down to look for lodgings. He has been seriously ill, and is still in a very anxious state. He had a great fancy to come here, where he was so comfortable before, and my only objection was that there would be no room for me; but Mrs. Homer's being here settles the question. She is going to continue, I suppose?"

"She only knows herself, ma'am," said Mrs. Saffery; "she only stays from week to week, but I've no notion she thinks of leaving."

"I fancied she would want a cottage."

"She is always on the look-out for one, ma'am, and partly thinks of building."

"Dear! I should think she would never do that."

"Oh yes, ma'am, she's been in treaty for

land, and at one time things were nearly brought to a conclusion. She was much disappointed at not getting Nessy's cottage, and we were much obliged to you, ma'am, for thinking of us."

"I thought it might be a good thing for both parties," said Edith.

"And your name," said Mrs. Saffrey, "was quite a voucher. Indeed, it was the only one she gave, for we thought there was no need to ask for another; and we never knew till yesterday how slight your intimacy was, and that she had never seen Mr. Antony."

"Oh no," said Edith; "there was no chance of her doing so, for I only knew her when I was with Mrs. Crowe."

"Meaning the lady who kept the school you both went to, I suppose?" said Mrs. Saffery.

"Went to?" repeated Edith; "Why, Mrs. Crowe was her own mother."

"Oh, indeed!" said Mrs. Saffery, looking all curiosity; and Nessy, too, was anxious to hear more; seeing which, Edith went on without any reluctance :—

"Mrs. Homer's connexions are quite respectable, Mrs. Saffery. You need be under no uneasiness about that. Her father was an officer, who retired on half-pay soon after his marriage. He had several children, of whom only his eldest and youngest daughter survived. Mrs. Homer is the youngest. He was a very good sort of man, I have been told, but his health was quite mined by injuries received in battle. As he could leave his family no provision, Mrs. Crowe, on his death, opened a school."

"At Cromer, ma'am?"

"No, near Ipswich. But, Mrs. Saffery, can you direct me to any lodgings?"

"Well, ma'am, I wish I could, but really none occur to me. Wouldn't you like to take some refreshment, Miss Antony?"

"Thank you; I should like a slice of bread and butter very much," said Edith. "I meant to have brought some biscuits, but had not time. Perhaps I may find some place in the neighbourhood, where they will take us in."

"There's a nice, quiet inn, Miss Antony."

"Oh! that would be too expensive."

"I doubt very much whether you might not make some cheap arrangement."

"Well, I will look about the neighbourhood

first. My brother is not well enough to like the bustle of an inn."

"Step in here, Miss Antony, and Nessy shall bring the bread and butter directly."

Mrs. Saffery opened the door of Mrs. Homer's parlour, and Edith was about to enter, but she drew back.

"No," she said; "Mrs. Homer's letters and papers are lying about, and I should not like to intrude. I should not like such a liberty taken with *me*."

"Come into our own little parlour, then, Miss Antony, if you don't mind."

"Not at all; I am very much obliged to you. Ah, Nessy—Miss Saffery! there are your pictures on the wall."

"Please call me 'Nessy,' ma'am, if you've no objection."

"Then you must not call me 'ma'am;' it sounds so dreadfully formal. How are you getting on with your painting?"

"Oh! not at all, at present. It has been quite set aside for other things."

"Women *must* set aside the fine arts pretty often for other things, if they are true women," said Edith; "and my brother says that is one of the reasons why they are seldom or never good artists. Do you remember that sketch he took the last time we went to Dulwich?"

"Oh, yes!" said Nessy, laughing; "when you drew the cow lowing for her calf."

"And you the cow with the crumpled horn. A professional gentleman of some eminence saw that sketch of my brother's the other day, and commissioned a cabinet-picture of the same subject, to which he is to give the nicest finish. That is why he wants to come here instead of going to the sea."

At this moment the shop-bell tinkled, and Nessy went to attend the summons. Farmer Benson came in, and said, in rather a dissatisfied voice—

"Oh! good morning, miss. Can you give me a notion, now, whether that lady-lodger of yours has made up her mind yet about that piece of ground?"

"Mrs. Homer isn't at home, Mr. Benson, but I'll tell her you want her answer."

"Because, you see, another party's about it, and between two stools I may fall to the ground. Is she going to keep on here?"

"We don't know in the least," said Nessy.

"Because she's been sounding my good dame times oft about letting her come to our *fiarm*, and my mistress, you see, wouldn't say yes; but now she's thought it over a bit, and our Betsy's gone to Yarmouth, and won't be back for a month at least; so that if that would suit Mrs. Homer, you may tell her that, if she will, she may."

"Yes, I will," said Nessy, quickly; "but there's a lady in our parlour now, Mr. Benson, who has come down from London to look for country lodgings, so that if they do not suit one, they may the other."

"Ho!" said he, deliberatively. Then, lowering his voice, "What sort of lady, now, may she be?"

"I will ask her to speak to you," said Nessy. "She is sister to Mr. Antony, who lodged here in the spring, and painted so beautifully."

"Oh! I mind *him* well enough," said the farmer. "He was continually hanging about my premises at one time, and I thought he was after mischief, till I came to warn him off, and then I found he was an artist."

"Miss Antony, will you speak to Farmer Benson, please?" said Nessy. "He has some nice lodgings, and Mr. Antony knows his farm-house, and used to admire it."

Edith came out, and her fair, frank face won the farmer's impressible heart directly.

"I know, miss, that if we please you, you'll please us," said he, cheerfully. "I can see it at a glance. We know your brother, my missis and me, and will do the best we can for you."

"But about Mrs. Homer?" said Edith, who had heard the previous dialogue; "must not she decide first?"

"Yes, she must decide first, if she *will* decide," said the farmer; "but she is a very undecideable person, and I don't see why I should go and miss selling my land, and miss letting my lodgings too, because she *will* keep shilly-shally."

"Then, perhaps," said Edith, "I may as well see your lodgings; and then, if they suit, and Mrs. Homer does not want them, we . can engage them. If Mrs. Homer takes them, my brother can come here."

"Just it," said he. "You step down to my fiarm—Daisylands Fiarm—and see Mrs. Ben-son, and you and she will settle everything, I'll answer for it, as far as can be settled."

"It would have been as well to know Mrs. Homer's mind first," observed Edith, "because, if she decides on your farm, it would save me the trouble of going there."

"She doesn't know her *own* mind, mum, I'm thinking."

"Mrs. Homer is at Mrs. Weir's," said Nessy, "but she will return to dinner; and you will have time, meanwhile, to see the rooms at Daisylands. It is a pretty walk; shall I show you the way?"

"Yes, do, for I always feel out of my element in the country," said Edith.

"Yes, that's well planned, Miss Saffery," sai Farmer Benson. "I'm going over to Kingston, but you just tell my dame what we've been saying, and she'll take the matter up where I leave it. I shall hear the upshot when I come home, it so being you can get Mrs. Homer to say one thing or the other. She's mighty pretty; but as for business—" And with a shrug and a smile he took leave.

Nessy hastened to tell her mother she was going to show Miss Antony the way to Daisylands, and was soon ready for the walk. They chatted pleasantly all the way; and Nessy told her friend what an interesting occupation she found her Sunday class. "It gives me something to think of all the week," said she, "and makes me brush up all the little knowledge I have, and wish for more."

"I dare say it does that," said Edith, "though I never undertook anything of the kind myself. A good, zealous, stirring clergyman never happened to cross my path."

"*We* never had one till now," said Nessy, "and it makes such a difference! His sermons give one something to think of all the week."

When they came to the hilly field, she told Edith of Mrs. Weir's fright, and Mrs. Homer's coming to her assistance. "They have been very intimate ever since," said she.

"Well, I should never have thought of Mrs. Homer's being at the trouble of rescuing *any* old lady," said Edith. "It speaks well for her. I suppose she saw there was no real danger."

"I think Mrs. Homer very amiable," said Nessy timidly.

"Do you?" said Edith. Nessy wished and yet dreaded to hear what she would add; but she added nothing.

"Oh, what a pretty old farmhouse beneath the slope! What splendid hollyhocks!"

"That's Daisylands," said Nessy, gladly. "I knew you would like it."

Edith liked it, and everything belonging to it, very much; and Mrs. Benson liked *her*, and remembered Mr. Antony, and was glad to see Nessy, and renewed her husband's invitation to have a syllabub at the farm "some of these days." A syllabub party, with Mr. and Miss Antony for two of its members, would indeed be very pleasant.

CHAPTER XX.

COUNTRY LODGINGS.

MRS. HOMER had undertaken to insert the
variegated pines in the white stripes of Mrs.
Weir's Affghan blanket; and, as this was a
task which Mrs. Weir had no mind for herself,
though she liked very well to knit the plain
stripes of yellow, green, and scarlet, she gladly
retained her till near dinner-time, and then
begged her to stay. Mrs. Homer consented,
on condition that she might run home and
fetch her cap.

Now, this cap was not a little muslin skull-
cap, with three heavy sausages of white muslin
round the front, and long, broad-hemmed strings,
like Mrs. Weir's, but an airy little fabric of
French blonde, light as the gossamer that floats
in summer air. Mrs. Homer had gone into a
slighter stage of mourning very soon after her
taking possession of the Safferys' lodgings ; and

Mrs. Saffery had made use of the circumstance to express a hope that the lady was becoming a little more reconciliated to her loss; but had been checked by, "There are some bereavements, Mrs. Saffery, too sacred to approach."

But now, though she wore deep and very becoming mourning, to wit, rich black silk, trimmed with crape, her cap, as above described, was of the lightest, and concealed very little of her beautiful, silky, dark hair, banded *à la Madonna.*

Returning, then, for her cap, she heard, with some surprise, and certainly without any manifestation of pleasure, from Mrs. Saffery, that Miss Antony had called to inquire if the lodgings were vacant.

"Of course you told her they were *not,*" said Mrs. Homer, with emphasis.

"Do you mean to continue in occupation then, ma'am?"

"Most certainly. Do you wish me to leave?"

"Oh no, ma'am, no! Only as you only continue by the week, I thought I should like to know whether there was any certainty of continuance. If you left, which I'm sure, ma'am, we should regret, Mr. Antony would come in, that's all."

"I do mean to continue."

"Thank you, ma'am. I'm sure our desire is to make you comfortable to the utmost of our means."

"I'm quite satisfied, Mrs. Saffery" (with one of her sweet forgiving smiles); "you are good creatures!"

"Mr. Benson called while you was away, ma'am," pursued Mrs. Saffery, after a pause, "and wished to know if you wanted *his* lodgings."

"Oh! You should have told me that in the first instance. Of course I cannot take them, now that I have pledged myself to you. I thought Mrs. Benson did not choose to let lodgings."

"Her daughter being gone on a visit, ma'am, she is willing to let her rooms for a month."

"A month! Oh, that is no time at all! It would not be worth while to remove for only a month."

"No, ma'am, that's what I was thinking, and that's what made it slip my memory at first. I thought, 'Mrs. Homer wouldn't care to go for a month.'   And the end of it would bring you into November, when the weather mostly breaks up; and them lanes is *very* dirty.   And so Nessy has took Miss Antony to see them."

"Oh, the Antonys want the lodgings at Daisylands, do they?"

"Not if you want them, ma'am.   If you stay here, they'll go there.   If you go there, they'll come here.   Miss Antony's quite agreeable."

Mrs. Homer seemed put out.   "The Antonys could not come here," said she, abruptly, "for you could not accommodate them both."   Then, after a little thought, "I mean to stay here."

"Thank you, ma'am, I thought you would. You are nearer the church, and the school, and Mrs. Weir—and *at* the post-office.   And you can be here as long as you like, and you could only be a month at Daisylands, which will be long enough for Mr. and Miss Antony.   Farmer Benson left word particular, that he wanted your answer, ma'am, no or yes, about the land, because another party is about it."

"I dare say that is only an excuse.   However, I will write to him in the evening; I cannot stay now, because I am going to dine with Mrs. Weir."

And, with her cap in a dainty little covered basket, she was lightly threading her way back, when she met Edith and Nessy, and greeted the former in pretty surprise.

"Miss Antony! Edith!—what pleasure!—are you come to stay? are you come to see me?"

"No," said Edith, "I did not know where you were, and came down about Mrs. Saffery's lodgings; but I have just seen some which will do equally well if you are not going to move."

"Do *you* wish me to move?"

"Oh, no; I prefer the Daisyland lodgings of the two, if you do not want them; they are so much more countrified."

"They *are* much more countrified; they are *much* preferable in situation; and I tried so for them!—you *know* I did, Miss Saffery. But Mrs. Benson would not hear of it; I don't think she liked my mournful face; and now she has come to terms just as I have pledged myself to Mrs. Saffery!"

"Oh, my mamma would not let that stand in the way, I'm sure," interposed Nessy, "if you really wished to go to Daisylands; and we could have Mr. Antony."

Mrs. Homer's smile of sweetness said plainly as words, "*Quite* out of the question." "My pledge is given," repeated she ; "I cannot think of departing from it. But, Miss Antony, shall I turn back with you ?—Most unfortunately I am engaged to dine with Mrs. Weir, but *do* let me give it up."

"On no account," said Edith, smiling. "What would Mrs. Weir think of you ? Your pledge is given."

"Oh, but I would explain—I would take it on myself—I would say, a friend from London—"

"Oh no, no, thank you. Since you decide on remaining at Mrs. Saffery's, I shall engage the Daisylands lodgings, and return at once to London."

"But *do* have a good rest first in my little retreat—have a little bread and fruit—have a glass of milk—have a glass of wine—lie down on the couch, or on my bed—"

"Oh no, no, thank you !—"

"How sorry I am—so unfortunate.—Well, we shall soon meet again, and then I hope we shall see much of each other. A mere step will divide us ; and if there should be anything I can do—"

"Thank you.   Good-bye."

"*Good*-bye !—So glad you're coming."

Each took her separate way, and, as Edith went onward, she said almost inaudibly, "don't believe it;" which made Nessy start.

"That young lady who came down with you last time," said she, after a little silence ; "is she quite well ?"

"Miss Bell, do you mean ? She may be quite well—most likely is. To tell the truth, I don't much care whether she is well or not."

Again Nessy was astounded.

"In fact," resumed Edith, "I think a severe illness might do her good. It would make her feel ; and if she felt suffering herself, she might come to feel for others."

"Is she rather unfeeling, then ?" said Nessy.

"Rather," said Edith, with bitter emphasis. "I dare say you saw what attention my brother paid her."

"Oh, yes ! I thought—my mamma thought they were engaged to be married."

"Ah ! I thought so too, when we went home that afternoon ; and so did my brother ; but it was all illusion. She was a heartless girl. She had drawn him on at first, accepted his attentions, and so forth, and actually made a false excuse that day, to be allowed to come with us —which I did not know till we were in the train. She had told them at home she was going to spend the day with *me*. Not a word about my brother, or the Dulwich Gallery, you understand."

" That was very deceiving of her," said Nessy.

" Persons who will deceive in a small thing, will deceive in a great one," said Edith. " You never can depend on them. She deceived my brother. She liked his admiration as long as she had no one else to admire her ; she let him think she would marry him, though against the wishes of her friends. And directly she had the offer of a richer match, she threw him overboard."

" Oh, how base of her," exclaimed Nessy. " I hope Mr. Antony did not mind it much. She did not deserve he should."

"Mind it ? Why, he had a brain fever ! " said Edith. " He fancied her a very superior creature to what she was ; dressed her up in all sorts of imaginary virtues and attractions, and was as bitterly disappointed as if she had really possessed them. He was very ill indeed,

Nessy, and had no one to nurse him except me and an old servant. You cannot think how unhappy I was. One night, he was delirious, and I thought he would die. I told you this morning, that I had never happened to know a good clergyman. You cannot think how, during my brother's illness, I wished for a visit from some good clergyman."

"Such as Mr. Weir," said Nessy. "How he would have comforted you!"

"I was thinking chiefly of my brother," said Edith. "He was, or seemed to me, on the very brink of another world; and, when there was an opportunity of saying a nice word or two, I did not in the least know what to say to him. However, as soon as the fever began to pass off, he made light of it—pretended nothing was the matter with him—and there was no opportunity of speaking to him *then*. And then he took cold, before he was well out of the fever, and it settled on his lungs; and he was sadly wilful and wayward, and *would* do imprudent things . . . so you may imagine what a time I have had. He is dreadfully altered."

"If Miss Bell could see him now—" said Nessy.

"There is no Miss Bell, now," said Edith, smiling sadly; "she is Mrs. Major Spinks."

"Well, perhaps it is best so," said Nessy; "for now he knows she is completely out of his reach. . . I am so sorry Mr. Antony is ill," she added, with feeling. "If he had come to our lodgings, I am sure my mamma would have nursed him as if he had been her son; but perhaps it is a good thing he will go to Daisylands, for the air is certainly better, and they say the breath of cows and the smell of freshly-ploughed earth are wholesome ; and the men are ploughing there now. And he can have new milk, and curds and whey, and new-laid eggs, and poultry ; and Mrs. Benson is very kind, and has had great experience, so that I don't believe you could go to a better place. I saw that Mrs. Benson took to you at first sight, and she *must* like Mr. Antony."

Edith smiled. "I fancy that we shall be comfortable there," said she. "Do you know, it will be a positive treat to me, to sleep in a room with a lattice-window ! And that blackbird in its wicker cage is a great attraction. There are bee-hives too, and a sun-dial. Oh ! I think we have a pleasant month in store ;

and if my brother gets on well with his picture, it will put the faithless Rosabel out of his head. That fanciful name is just a sample of his way of idealizing things. Just as he converted Rosa Bell into Rosabel, so did he convert a very silly, commonplace, trumpery girl, into a personification of all that was good and worthy to be loved."

Here they reached the post-office, and Nessy said, "I don't know where Mrs. Homer's fruit was to come from, Miss Antony, for there is not even an apple in the house; but it is near our dinner-time, and if you don't mind hashed mutton, I am sure my papa and mamma will be very much honoured by your dining with us."

"Oh, I shall be home by *our* dinner-time, thank you," said Edith; "and you know I have lunched already. As to 'bread and fruit,' that is such an old, familiar sentimentalism of Mrs. Homer's, that I could hardly help laughing when I heard it again. I am not at all surprised at her offering it when she knew very well there was no fruit in the cupboard. She was wonderfully fond, when a girl, of saying she should delight in living on bread and fruit,

or bread and honey; but she had her fair share
of beef and mutton all the same."

Mrs. Homer, on returning to Mrs. Weir's,
found Mrs. Fownes calling on her; and as
Mrs. Fownes had for some time had her eye on
the interesting young widow, and wondered
where she came from and what she was going
to do, she was very glad to hear all Mrs. Weir
had to tell about her. This was little enough,
as regarded her antecedents, but Mrs. Weir
made a capital story of her fright in the hilly
field, and Mrs. Homer's self-devotion in staying
by her when she might have run away; and
warming with her subject, she praised her so
heartily, that Mrs. Fownes was prepossessed in
her favour. Therefore, when Mrs. Homer came
in, she condescended to be introduced to her,
and to speak to her kindly; and after a few
remarks exchanged, she said,

"I hear you are looking out for a cottage in
this neighbourhood. Have you seen Tresellis?"

Mrs. Homer had neither seen it nor heard of
it, but she was captivated by the name.

"Let me recommend you to go and look
at it, then," said Mrs. Fownes. "It is not on
any road, so that you would not be likely to

see it if you were not looking for it. I have
not been there myself; but we came upon it
one day when the doctor and I were driving,
and took the wrong lane by mistake, and I
thought it a pity that such a pretty little place
should be getting out of repair for want of an
occupant. I remember the Doctor's quoting
the first verse of Edwin and Emma. I dare
say you know it—

> " 'Far in the windings of a vale,
> Fast by a sheltering wood,
> The safe retreat of health and peace,
> A rustic cottage stood.' "

"Oh, I should like such a place *so* much,"
said Mrs. Homer, pressing her hands closely
together. "I so long for a home."

"It is very secluded."

"Oh, seclusion is what I want!"

"Is that quite a healthy feeling for so young
a person? Heavy griefs are apt to make us
feel we can take no more interest in this world;
but we have duties to fulfil in it till we are
taken out of it."

Mrs. Homer's expressive look replied that
that question had been considered in every
point of view already.

" Would Tresellis be an expensive place to keep up?" said she presently.

" I don't know what repairs it may need," said Mrs. Fownes. " Probably white washing and papering, and a little carpentering; but, supposing it in tenantable repair, I should say that any one with two hundred a-year might live there in perfect comfort."

" Oh, then, it is *quite* within my reach," said Mrs. Homer. After a little silence, she said, " I have two hundred a year that came to me in a singular manner, quite independent of other resources. 'Tis a romantic little story. I am sure I might confide it to such kind, judicious friends—if they found any interest in it."

They both assured her, with sincerity, they should listen with lively interest. She drooped her eyelids, and never once looked up, while she gave the following details with charming simplicity.

" 'Tis now some little time back, that a worthy man, one of the excellent of the earth, fixed his too-partial regards on me. What he could see in me to admire, I can't conceive: you know, there's no accounting for these things. He fancied he could be happy with me—wished to marry me. My family, my friends, wished so too; but I did not—one *cannot* always rule the heart. Yet there was so much, in the ordinary point of view, to be said in favour of it, that I was—oh! so nearly persuaded! 'Tis sweet, you know, to sacrifice one's self for those one loves. So, in fact, I was on the very brink of this sacrifice—a mere child at the time—without one bit of heart in it, scarce knowing I had one, when he was carried off by a sudden seizure, and the sacrifice was spared."

"Dear me!" exclaimed both the ladies; "and have you worn widow's mourning for *him?*"

"Excuse me; no," said Mrs. Homer, with a mournful shake of the head. "1 put on deep mourning for him, but not that of a widow. Will you believe it? this exemplary man, with the providence—the prevision—which marked his character, had settled two hundred per annum on me, whether our union took place or not."

"Dear me!" again ejaculated the old ladies.

"That showed great attachment to you," said Mrs. Fownes.

" Oh ! ——" And Mrs. Homer looked un-utterable things.

" It made a great noise at the time," she softly added. " Everybody admired him : pitied or envied me. They little understood me ! "

" And then, you married . . . ."

" The subject becomes too painful," said she, covering her eyes with her white hand. " This world is *full* of sorrows. My heart is still too lacerated . . . Dear Mrs. Weir, shall I trouble you for the yellow wool ? "

Meanwhile, Nessy, continuing to hover about Miss Antony as long as she possibly could, gathered her a nosegay, and as Edith was already laden with some of Mrs. Benson's new-laid eggs and a bottle of cream, Nessy begged to be allowed to carry them to the station.

" Yes, do, Nessy," said her mother. " We will put you by some dinner."

" Oh, never mind my dinner," said Nessy, supremely happy. On their way to the station, they found plenty to talk about; and among other things, Nessy ventured to ask Miss Antony if she had done anything new lately in the way of authorship.

"Oh, that has been completely set aside," said Edith, smiling. "I forgot you knew I had ever made any attempts of the kind. Authorship requires leisure and a quiet mind. Perhaps, when I come down here, I may make a new start."

"I'm sure I hope you will," said Nessy. "I think a book of your writing would be one of the nicest that ever was read."

They reached the station only a few minutes before the train came up; and remained chatting on the platform. Nessy expressed her wonder whether Mrs. Homer would stay with them through the winter. She hoped she would.

"I must say I hope she will not," said Edith, "though it is no matter of mine. She has duties to fulfil somewhere else. It was a sentimental, mistaken thing, her coming here, where she can be of no manner of use."

"She is rather useful in the school now," suggested Nessy, "though I don't think she thoroughly likes it. In that case, there is the more merit in her persevering as she does."

"Keeping up one's Scriptural knowledge must always be good," said Edith, "and I suppose Sunday classes must at least do that. Here comes the train! Good-bye. Mind the cream!"—

"I'll give it you when you are in."

A little delay occurred after Edith had taken her seat; and they continued talking.

"This will be to Leonard a specimen of the productions of the promised land," said Edith, cheerfully. "I feel the better even for this short treat. 'Living on air' has a different meaning here.'"

"I suppose we shall see you often, Mrs. Homer being with us," said Nessy.

"Oh, I don't think I shall trouble *her* with much of my company. But I shall come to post our letters."

"Mrs. Homer's trial may have made her give way a little too much," said Nessy, anxious to raise her favourite in Miss Antony's good graces, "but I suppose her husband was a great loss—"

"'*Was?*'" repeated Edith. The whistle shrieked, the train moved on, and there was not time for another word.

END OF VOL. I.

LONDON:
R. CLAY, SON, AND TAYLOR, PRINTERS,
BREAD STREET HILL.

BENTLEY'S POPULAR WORKS.

One Shilling and Sixpence.
TALES FROM BENTLEY. Vols. 1, 2, 3, and 4.

Two Shillings and Sixpence.
WHAT TO DO WITH THE COLD MUTTON. Third Thousand.

EVERYBODY'S PUDDING BOOK; or, Puddings, Tarts. &c. for all the year round. Third Thousand.

THE LADY'S DESSERT BOOK. By the Author of "Everybody's Pudding Book."

NELLY ARMSTRONG. A Story of Edinburgh Life.

THE SEMI-DETACHED HOUSE. Edited by Lady Theresa Lewis.

THE SEMI-ATTACHED COUPLE. By the same Author.

THE LADIES OF BEVER HOLLOW. By the Author of "Mary Powell."

VILLAGE BELLES. By the same Author.

EASTON. By Hon. Lena Eden.

THE SEASON TICKET.

NOTES ON NOSES. By Eden Warwick.

SAY AND SEAL. By the Author of "Wide, Wide World."

Four Shillings.
DR. M'CAUSLAND'S SERMONS IN STONES; or, Scripture confirmed by Geology. Tenth Thousand.

LADY CHATTERTON'S TRANSLATIONS FROM PLATO.

JULIA KAVANAGH'S MADELINE: a Tale of Auvergne. Gilt edges.

Five Shillings.
THE INGOLDSBY LEGENDS; or, Mirth and Marvels. Sixty-eighth Thousand.

FRANCATELLI'S COOK'S GUIDE. 100 Recipes and 40 Woodcuts. Nineteenth Thousand.